Suicide Blonde

canon doyle

NEW PULP PRESS

Published by New Pulp Press, LLC, 926 Truman Avenue, Key West, Florida 33040, USA.

For information contact:
Publisher@NewPulpPress.com

Printed in the United States of America
Visit us on the web at www.newpulppress.com

Suicide Blonde

Chapter One

The name is Stone ... Axis Stone, occupation private detective, you know somebody says follow that dude, so I follow him, somebody says find a missing chick, so I find her and what do I get out of it? Fifty bucks an hour and expenses and if you think that buys anything fancy these days then you're from outer space – it's a labor of love but if I want be honest – it's the only gig I feel comfortable doing ... You've probably heard about some of my cases on the news, well whatever you hear or you read, the real thing is something else ... and there's only one guy who knows that – I know it.

It was a stinking hot day outside. Sydney is like that at summer time. But my office is cool – in both ways. The chorus to the song *The Terrible Tango* cranked up and cut the tedium, it was the ringtone of my smartphone – one of my favorite songs. I searched for the phone under a pile of unpaid bills and credit card demands piled high on my desk – found it and put on my most congenial voice, hoping for a gig.

"Axis Investigations, Stone speaking."

A silky, breathy voice at the other end purred, "Mr. Stone, sorry I'm out of breath I was running to get out of the rain."

"Rain? You've got to be kidding!" I looked out of the window at the blue sky – there wasn't a cloud in it. "Are we on the same planet?" I challenged.

"I'm sorry Mr. Stone, I should have said I'm in Brisbane and it's pelting down cats and dogs."

"I see, miss ...?"

"Lola Lovejoy."

The name rang a bell. I'd seen it in the newspapers: nightclub singer Kitty Lovejoy kidnapped in some

1

exotic place – yeah, the Philippines that was it.

"Are you related to ...?"

"Kitty? Yes, she's my sister."

"So, what can I do for you Miss Lovejoy?"

"You know that she's missing in the Philippines, well we're having some difficulties dealing with the police in Manila, and the Australian Consulate there can only provide us with limited assistance and won't get involved with the kidnapping investigation."

"Yeah, that's their policy as I understand it. So, go on ... where do I come in?"

"My father is a prominent Brisbane identity and wants to keep our name out of the newspapers."

"A bit late for that isn't it?"

"No more I should say, what's been reported so far has already done some damage."

"So what's the bottom line Miss Lovejoy?"

"We need representation in the Philippines. Dad doesn't trust anyone there, so I contacted you."

"How did you find me?"

"On the net ... can you meet us in Brisbane for dinner tonight?" She asked tentatively.

"Email me an open date return ticket and credit my account with three hundred bucks and I'll be there."

~~~

The crud weather made the ninety-minute flight to Brisbane a turbulent affair but nothing that a couple of in-flight Scotch's couldn't settle. I must admit I don't get to fly up front often and I could get used to all the attention business class provided. I was sat next a businessman who by his demeanor and dress made a living out of being a bore. He only spoke to me once during the flight and his breath was so ripe I made sure there wouldn't be any more conversation by ignoring him. A sultry-looking girl with short dark hair and boobs about the size of tennis balls, the business class hostess, was pleasant enough but that's about as far as it went – even that ended with her smile. She was a walking advertisement for braces – could eat an apple through a tennis racket.

I decided to kill time by mentally undressing the girl across the aisle. Evaluating people was one of my routines – especially pretty girls. In her mid-twenties with shoulder length well-groomed blonde hair, dressed in an A-line summery pale blue floral print number that showed off both her cleavage and her long tanned legs, she was dressed to impress. The gold bangles on both wrists and the long beautifully manicured fingernails told me she was a model. I followed the line of her shapely legs down to her shoes, unmistakably Jimmy Choo – expensive. She caught me looking and loved it, the edges of her sexy red painted mouth rose with a clipped smile. I immediately checked her ring fingers knowing she would instinctively fiddle them if she was taken, but she wasn't wearing any. Instead she reached down, and as though she was reading me better than I her, slipped off her shoes and began gently massaging her feet. That pretty well did my head in – Mr. Happy sprang into action trying to fight his way out of my pants. So, by the time the plane landed at Brisbane airport I was as horny as hell. As we deplaned I got into position directly behind her and squeezed up tight enough for Mr. Happy to rub into the cleavage of her lovely rear end. Again she didn't mind at all and gently pushed back with her butt to make better contact. I pulled a business card and slipped it to her. She took it with a silent wink. It pays to advertise.

~~~

Waiting at the airport cab rank, I was setting my wristwatch back an hour for daylight saving, when in my periphery vision I was struck by a pair of red, Luis

Vuitton open toed, high-heel shoes. I followed the shapely, tanned legs up to find a real honey: the sort you'd prefer to spread on a bed than on bread. A strawberry blonde with wide-spaced blue eyes and garbed in a thin silk dress that clung to her slim, well-proportioned body like paint to a wall – only a wall is a flat surface. This dame even surpassed the blonde on the plane.

"Mr. Stone?"

"All yours."

"Lola Lovejoy."

Her husky voice matched her name – Lola was a stunner – the gig was getting better by the second.

"I have a car waiting ... follow me."

"No problem at all," I purred with a grin like a Cheshire cat.

The goods looked just as impressive from behind. A dapper uniformed chauffeur held open the door to the white Mercedes C-class stretch limo, and I followed Lola inside. I sat down opposite her and she handed me an iPad.

"Here, everything you need to know, except your orders and payment details. We'll discuss those over dinner."

"Do I get to keep this?" I took the device and began reading.

"No," she said crossing her long tanned bare legs.

The next time I looked up, we were pulling into the driveway of a mansion.

"This your place?"

"No, Daddy's."

The Lovejoy estate was kept in immaculate condition. Trimmed green lawns ran off in all directions, neatly dotted with carefully shaped flowerbeds, where all the flowers grew strictly to attention. The house itself was a rambling structure, maybe fifty years old, but it gleamed from the obvious, and lavish, application of care and money.

~~~

Unfamiliar with the high-life, I felt like a fish out of water in the swanky dining room. A table set for three that could comfortably sit thirty-three. A butler with way too much starch in his shirt and the coat hanger still left in his suit coat, showed me a seat.

"Can I get you a drink sir?" He said with a plum in his mouth.

It felt like a scene out of A Night at the Opera.

"Yeah Jeeves, make it a Harvey Wallbanger." It was my preferred social drink.

"How's that sir?"

I fired him a single raised eyebrow figuring the recipe came with his suit. "Freshly squeezed orange juice, two fingers of vodka, a jig of Galliano, ice, a slice of orange only, no vegetation and stir don't shake."

"As you wish sir."

"As I wish, if I'd known it was a wish I'd have asked for three of them."

He ignored my wit and moved off stiffly and on his way out of the room passed an old guy suited up and balding, striding into the room as though he owned it. He propped in front of me and offered me his hand.

"Mr. Stone, Winston Lovejoy, please sit, Lola will join us directly."

"Nice pad you've got here Winston. You're a high court judge aren't you?"

"Yes, have you read the case file?"

"Ah ha, but I couldn't get the drift as to why Kitty was kidnapped, and why there's been no ransom demand."

"Now you can see our problem."

Just then Lola floated in like on a cloud. The complete package: she could cause a room full of

5

Parkinson's patients to stop shaking.

We stood for her to sit.

"Lola, Mr. Stone was asking why there has been no ransom demand."

"That has us worried too Mr. Stone," she purred like panther.

"Look, I've never been to the Philippines so it's unfamiliar turf for me. Bottom line is, I make a practice of not taking on more than I can chew."

"Your frankness is commendable Stone – Lola has confidence in you and I trust her judgment."

"So what is it you want from me?"

Lola and the old boy exchanged a glance. She took the reins.

"We want you to go to Manila to be our eyes and ears on what the police know and are doing."

"I can't guarantee I'll be able to ..."

Winston butted in. "We're not asking you find Kitty, just monitor the investigation," he growled a little testily.

"If you find yourself in the position to rescue her, then fine, but that's not the brief," Lola corrected.

"I see. This is because you're getting little from them?"

"Nothing would be more like it!" The old man cackled. I could see he was getting uptight. "Look Stone," he snapped. "I've exhausted all my connections trying to get information, but we can't find out a damned thing!" His face had turned red and he was puffing up like he was about to explode.

"Dad, take it easy, calm down. He has a bad heart. The stress of this is killing him. I'll take him up to his room, meet me in the drawing room, there's a bar there, help yourself."

She was speaking my kind of language. I watched her help the old boy out of the room then went for a wander to find the drawing room and more so, the bar.

A couple of minutes later Lola was comfortably established in an armchair at one end of the fancy drawing room, a glass of Scotch in her hand, while I sat on a leather couch facing her nursing a bourbon on the rocks.

She'd changed her clothes. Whoever the guy was who created the silver lame sheath she wore with such elegance, he was not only a master of design, I realized appreciatively, but a miser with material, too. The sheath was sleeveless for a start, and when she crossed her legs the hem automatically hiked a good four inches above her knees. The entire creation was supported by fragile shoulder straps the width of her little finger, and the scooped neckline had the good taste to realize that even silver lame couldn't compete with a substantial expanse of majestic cleavage, and didn't try.

"Dad's aged since this all started with Kitty," she said dispiritedly.

"I can dig that," I got up and walked over to the open fireplace that wasn't alight. As a matter of fact it being Brisbane, I wondered whenever it would be cold enough to light it. A mirror on the mantle caused me to assess myself. Short-cropped mousey brown hair that needed a trim, same for my three days growth – reminiscent of Jamie Dornan, I thought, only after a big night out on the booze. Still, women love me, while most guys see me as a threat – anyhow, who gives a rats? – I repeat – women love me.

"See anyone you know Mr. Stone?"

I turned and faced her. "I see a guy with plenty to think about."

She took a sip of her Scotch then shrugged her smooth bare shoulders in a quick movement, as if she wished she could shrug off any doubts.

"Oh, I think you'll make the right decision. You

seem to be the kind of guy that embraces a challenge."

She got that right, the embrace part. I sat back down and drained my bourbon.

"Mind if I have a nightcap?"

She leaned forward in the chair and looked at me earnestly, "Help yourself, Mr. Stone."

"Does that only go for the drink?" I quipped.

"Goes without saying that a man like you should know how to help himself, shouldn't he?"

"Comes with the license lady," I said pouring myself three fingers of rye.

"Is it fringe benefits you're enquiring about Mr. Stone?"

Returning to the couch I said, "If you don't ask you don't get ... that is my motto Miss Lovejoy."

"Well, we might save that one until we know each other a little better," she sighed gently, tactfully sidestepping the innuendo of our little tête-à-tête. She placed her glass still half full, as I would see it, on the coffee table and then stood with great poise.

"Your bedroom is the first left on the upstairs landing. Breakfast on the balcony at 8 A.M., sharp. You'll find pajamas on your bed and all you need in the en-suite bathroom. Goodnight Mr. Stone."

"Right." I shot her a grateful smile. *What a broad,* I mumbled to myself.

Chapter Two

Two days later I was in first class sipping champagne on a Qantas flight from Sydney to Manila.

I'd arranged to be collected at Manila airport by a local PI, Ricky Esposo. I found him at arrivals holding a card under his chin with my surname on it.

We got to know each other as we crawled along in infamous Manila traffic on route to my hotel in Makati. I'd not seen traffic like it.

A stocky little bloke with a razor sharp wit we got on like a house on fire.

He drove his late model white Corolla up to the fancy entrance of the Shangri-La Hotel and I was impressed, a top shelf joint – little guys in white uniforms surrounded the car to open doors and take my bags, I felt like King Farouk. After I checked-in I took Ricky up to my room to discuss the case and it didn't take me long to get how switched on his was – I guess it comes with the territory.

"So Ricky, what's the dope on the Kitty Lovejoy fiasco?"

"Well, Mister Stone, there's not much to tell: she came to Manila a year ago contracted as lounge singer at the Captain's Bar in the Mandarin Oriental Hotel: the top lounge bar in the Philippines. That's where she met Buddy Nelson, the American owner of Dawn Talent Agency in Makati. He provides plenty of artists work in television commercials and local movies as well as booking singers into a number of clubs. He got her plenty of work. Filipino's like her sexy movie star look. She starred in a few notable television commercials – then she got a residency at 71 Gramercy Bar Lounge in Century City, the numero uno upmarket nightclub in Makati."

"Was that through Nelson as well?"

"Don't know boss ... after that she was in all the social pages a lot with known local gangster Ringo Raye – he owns Gramercy. "

Ricky handed over his iPhone. "The venue poster."

I checked the photo – a hot redhead in a slinky red evening dress that titillated the imagination, standing on stage next to a grand piano. Then it struck me like a ton of bricks.

"That's Lola!"

"No boss, that's Kitty."

"She's got a sister, they must be identical twins!"

I needed to check out the abduction details. Ricky had all the newspaper articles but I wanted to hear from someone closer the victim. Ricky suggested Kitty's PA, a Filipina with the unusual name of Chicki Dee. He took me to her condo in Fort Bonifacio: a suburb of Makati.

~~~

Ricky waited in the car while I rang the intercom. After I'd explained myself the sexy accented voice invited me up.

~~~

The apartment door opened to a sexy little suntanned thing in a pink robe.

"Hi, are you?"

"Chicki Dee, please come in Mr. Stone."

It was a small modern apartment with scant furnishings. She sat on the three-seat lounge and drew her legs up. The front of her robe inadvertently dropped open enough for me to catch sight of a lovely breast. She caught me looking and shut the gate.

"How can I help you?" She said curtly.

Right now she could help me most by dropping the robe – it had been a while.

"You were with Kitty when she was abducted?"

"Yes, we were in the Century City car park after the performance when ..."

She burst into tears.

I leapt out of the armchair, sat beside her and placed my arm around her shoulders to comfort her like every white knight is supposed to. She suddenly submitted to my embrace, whimpering like a baby. After a few minutes of consoling we were kissing passionately – the robe had been discarded and I was buck naked. I came up in back of her and leaned forward, my hands cupping her breasts, the thumbs gently flicking her flaccid nipples. My now fully erect rod firmly pressed against the deep cleft of her bottom, and my thighs were tight against the back of her thighs.

"Oh that feels so good," she moaned.

"Likewise," I agreed, then nibbled her right carlobc.

There was a distant roll of thunder, and then lightning split the sky.

"Don't you love it," I said. "Nature providing a score for us ... are you ready for me?"

I slid my cock gently into her warm moist haven and she bent even more forward, thrusting her rounded cheeks hard against me. There was more thunder, closer this time, followed by another jagged streak of lightning, the rhythm quickened between us. The storm had excited her. There was neither expertise nor technique. She rode my rod with a kind of wild abandon and climaxed a couple of minutes later. I followed her example a second later. Thunder and lightning missed their cues but you can't have everything. We came apart slowly, and then she turned and put her arms around my neck so her breasts pressed hard against my chest.

It had been fiery sex. She was unbelievable. Only a small girl, she had beautiful full breasts and a silky little strip of hair that highlighted the entrance to her moist slit. Once she got started there was no stopping her, she made Mr. Happy sing like he hadn't in ages. Exhausted, we eventually settled back naked and sticky on the lounge.

"Do you always conduct interviews in that manner Mr. Stone?"

"No, but I could make a habit of it."

"No condom either."

"If I wanted to fuck plastic I'd buy a blow up doll."

Her satisfied eyes beamed a warm smile. I was beginning to appreciate the nuances of Asian women, being my first, if Chicki was anything to go by, then things were certainly looking up in the pleasure stakes here. She needed to freshen up. I watched the brown round orbs of her bottom wiggle as she went to the bathroom and then dressed.

When she came back moments later I decided to get back on track.

"So, what happened in the car park?"

"Oh, we were walking to the car when two masked men came out of the dark, pulled a hood over Kitty's head, and pushed her into a waiting car. Before I could do anything they sped out of the car park."

"Anything about them you recognize?"

"I don't know Mr. Stone. I'm very afraid. They had masks," she cried.

I dropped the subject to settle her down and got into talking about her. She opened up.

"Are you from here, I mean Makati?"

"No, I'm from Bicol in the province."

"Is that a town?"

"No Legazpi City is the town."

"How long have you been in Makati?"

"For nearly seven years now ... I've been with Kitty as her PA for a year, before that I was two years with

EDSA Shangri-La public relations and before that I finished a bachelor of communication at Eastern University in Manila which took four years."

"Clever girl, your family must be very proud of you."

"Did you leave your home town to do the course at University?"

"Um, " she looked sheepish. "I will be honest with you, I got into a little trouble at home which meant I needed to leave town."

"Oh, can I ask what that was?" Thinking that maybe it has something to do with Kitty's kidnapping.

"I got pregnant to a local boy, I was only just eighteen."

She hopped up, went to the bedroom, returned with a framed photograph and handed it to me. It was of her and a young boy.

"That is my son Carlo taken last year, he was six then."

"A good-looking lad, so is he in Bicol?"

"Yes, with my parents and my ten brothers and sisters."

"Ten! Is your father a primary producer?"

"No, he works at the council," she said not getting the gag. "I have been saving my money to send Carlo to a good school. It is very expensive in the Philippines you know."

"Don't you have public schools here?"

"Yes, but there are so many children there is no chance. If you want to get a start in life you must go to a good school and that will cost nearly one hundred thousand pesos a year."

"That's about two grand US, I guess a lot of money for you."

"Yes. I saved up a deposit from working. It took me three years but now I have enough to get him enrolled. I am going to Bicol in two days to pay the deposit."

"So you must be worried about Kitty, your savings must depend on having a job."

"Oh yes sir."

"So help me find her Chicki. Do you know this guy Nelson?"

"Yes, he's not a good man."

"Hmm, I see. Tell me something about what happened, anything."

She pulled a face like she was about to cry and pleaded, "But I don't know anything sir, honest."

I got up.

"Okay look, you have a think about it and I'll come back tomorrow same time and we'll talk some more ... and maybe a little more hanky panky," I said grinning amorously.

She gave me a warm smile ... I knew she had enjoyed her encounter with Mr. Happy. I left her with a gentle kiss ... as every white knight is expected to do.

~~~

I climbed into front seat of the car and woke Ricky up.

"Hey, sorry Ricky, I got carried away."

"No problem boss," he yawned. "Learn anything?"

"Yeah plenty, she's afraid to put the finger on the kidnapper's but knows something. I'll need to massage it out of her. We'll come back same time tomorrow."

"The storm has gone," Ricky said looking up at the rolling clouds. "We get one of those every day this time of year. It's the rainy season."

~~~

He drove me to the Shang. It was late – I was beat. Before I got out I asked him, "I'll need a Roscoe Ricky."

He produced a holster and gun from under the seat.

"I thought you'd ask. Here, but be careful boss, everyone in Manila carries a loaded gun – they shoot first ask questions later."

"Sounds dangerous."

"Is still a cowboy town ... well that's what a Yankee private dick once told me."

"I like you Ricky ... we'll make a top team. You go home and get some rest ... do you start early?"

"Not really boss ... but..."

"A man after my own heart ... meet me at 8.30 A.M., by the pool for breakfast."

I watched the Corolla snake down the driveway and then I cruised into the Shang. There was plenty to catch the eye in the busy lobby, seems the place that time of night is a bit of a hang for Manila socialites to strut their stuff.

International hotels are weird, the lobby is always busy but you rarely see anyone in the corridors. I always fancied that one-day I'd step into an elevator and find a honey to die for, on her own just hanging for a sexual fling for the night. I suppose it's a bit like wanting to be seated next to a sex siren on an international flight – you know, she's on her way to a porno convention in Miami or somewhere and wants to join the mile-high club for bragging rights before she gets there. But hell, with all the fights I've taken over the years, I'm still a mile-high virgin.

Chapter Three

Ricky joined me for breakfast by the Shangi-La pool. "Morning boss."

"Sit down Ricky, I've ordered you a coffee."

"Salamat po.

"What's that mean?"

"Thank you in Filipino," he said brightly. "Tagalog."

"Cool, you keep on teaching me, it'll do me good to learn something more than swear words in a foreign language," I joked.

"Okay boss ... so, where to today?"

"First port-of-call will be Mr. Nelson at the Dawn Agency."

It was tough leaving the beautiful bods in their string bikinis lazing about in deckchairs by the pool like lounge lizards but I had crooks to catch – besides I was sweating up a soup, and packing a pistol meant I couldn't remove my sports coat.

~~~

Ricky waited in the car while I went inside the Legazpi Village office building. I ignored the four flights of stairs to Dawn Agency and took the elevator.

Even then by the time I fronted the cute receptionist my armpits were leaking big time. The aircon felt mighty.

"Hi honey, I'd like a word with Buddy Nelson?"

She stood. I gave her the once over. Short but well endowed, a cute thing with blue and green streaks in her long black hair.

"Who is calling, sir?" She whispered and fluttered her eyelashes.

I gave her my best profile and announced huskily, "Axis Stone, private detective representing the Lovejoy family."

It worked, her body language said she wanted me and she reluctantly disappeared behind a partition and then returned seconds later to usher me into Nelson's office.

A large gruff man with a receding hairline, a gnarly face with jowls, Nelson offered me his big mitt to shake.

"How can I be of assistance Mr. Stone?" He said in with a southern USA accent.

"I presume you're up to speed on the Kitty Lovejoy kidnapping. I have a few questions."

"Fire away."

"Where were you the night she was taken?"

"At dinner with an actress ... why am I a suspect?"

"Just wiping your slate ... any idea why she was kidnapped?"

"Try asking her boyfriend Ringo Raye."

He was giving me bad vibes – wasn't to be trusted.

"You sound like you've got a bone to pick with Raye."

"You could say that, he pinched one of my stars."

"Where are you from?"

"I live down the street ... that's enough questions?"

"Cute," I stood and eyeballed him.

"Don't try and hardball me Stone, I've got a forty-five in my desk here to eradicate vermin like you. We're done. "

"For now Nelson ... by your attitude I'd say Louisiana."

"What's that supposed to mean Aussie?"

"You said it in one Nelson. How did Raye take your fuckin' star when you didn't even get her the Gramercy gig?"

I didn't wait for a reply, thought I just leave him with that thought and bailed out.

On the way out I gave the sexy broad at the front

desk my best wink. By her response I got the impression I was a big hit with the local talent and wondered if that was normal in this town for a reasonably young, virile, handsome foreigner.

~~~

When I got into the car I had to wake Ricky. I don't know how he can sleep in the car; I guess it's the aircon.

"Where to now boss?" He mumbled sleepily.

"I wanna talk to the cop in charge of the investigation."

"That'd be Sancho Cortez, he's the principal investigator for Task Force Shanghai."

On the way there I decided to pick Ricky's brain a little.

"Hey listen, it seems I'm getting the eye from pretty young Filipinos."

"You mean Filipinas boss."

"Yeah, is that normal for a guy like me?"

"They probably think you're Hugh Jackman boss, that's why girls here would be attracted to you."

"Hugh Jackman aye, hmm, Wolverine." I kicked back in the front passenger seat feeling pretty good about myself. "Yeah, I can see that."

~~~

We parked in San Antonio and walked a short distance from the car park to Police HQ.

"I wasn't impressed with Nelson, dig into his cupboard Ricky ... see if you can dig up any skeletons will you?"

"Will do boss. I know Cortez ... he's a mean mother. He won't like a foreigner digging about in his case ... be careful boss."

"I'm listening to you Ricky. But don't worry, I know how to handle cops with a chip on their shoulder, happens to me a lot back home, an occupational hazard."

"Not like this I think boss."

We got a cool reception from the Desk Sergeant when I asked for Cortez and he kept us waiting an hour before we were eventually called into his office. Lucky they had air conditioning or I would have cut out.

Cortez glared up at me from behind his desk like I was the next item up for auction that he had no interest in. No formalities.

With a snarl on his rugged face he declared, "I do not any have time for foreigners sticking their nose into police business."

We sat. He reminded me of Eli Wallach who played Tuco, a cool bad guy in the classic sixties spaghetti western The Good, the Bad and the Ugly. I returned serve.

"Is coming to talk with you sticking my nose into your business?"

"You've got five minutes Mr. Stone."

"The Lovejoy family wanted an update on the kidnapping, they're getting nothing from you, so they sent me over."

He lit a half smoked cigar and puffed a wad of smoke at me. It stank.

"We have heard nothing – no ransom demand. Forensics combed the crime scene and found nothing. The only witness won't talk."

"You're talking about Chicki Dee?" I croaked and coughed from the smoke.

"See you've done some homework at least – I'm impressed," he said cynically.

He was small in stature but like Ricky, a nugget. Medium length black hair parted at the side, with a couple of long stands that draped down over his left eye. A take-no-prisoners look in his eye, an acne scarred face with a constant scowl like someone had pinched his lunch money – uncannily Tuco.

"Suspects?" I asked.

"Only one, Ringo Raye."

"Motive?"

"The girl was cheating on him."

"You mean Kitty?"

"Yeah."

"Cheating on him with whom?"

"Nicholas Vargas the third, look, you're a private dick, go and do your own footwork, Kitty Lovejoy has form and so does Raye. There is nothing we can do here until there has been a ransom demand. You should know that if you are worth your fat fee."

The way he said that told me he was jealous of the money I made that he didn't. I expected that to be a problem in a place where corruption was the only real way for a cop to earn a crust. I stood and flicked him my card.

"I'd appreciate a call if you hear anything."

He glanced at it then dropped it irreverently on his desk. "I do not have the budget for making long distance calls."

"My local mobile number is on the back. I'm staying at the Shangri La."

"I know, room 677," he said smugly – a reminder that I was in *his* town and I was on *his* turf.

"Come on by and I'll buy you lunch."

"Okay, I will consider it."

"Is it fine for me to I have a word with Raye and Vargas?"

"Be my guest. Goodbye Mr. Stone ... Ricky."

As we made our way out the door he called out, "Stone, two things you should know. One, you shouldn't be packing a gun without a permit and two, be very, very careful, this isn't Sydney, di ba?"

"Have you ever seen The Good the Bad and the Ugly?"

I didn't wait for an answer.

~~~

On our way to the car I asked Ricky, "What's di ba mean?"

"Slang Tagalog for *is it* – he said *this is not Sydney is it ...*"

"Okay, I figured it was something like that. I guess you were right this sure isn't Sydney."

~~~

I was deep in thought all the way back to Makati when an idea came to me.

"Ricky, where can we find this Nicholas Vargas bloke?"

"Probably the Manila Yacht Club."

"Good, let's go there for lunch."

"But you're not a member boss."

"Don't worry, I'd put money on Vargas being one."

The traffic was so bad it took an hour before we parked outside the classy club on Roxas Boulevard facing Manila Bay. Ricky wasn't sold on me getting us in. I enjoyed the challenge and backed myself. I guess I lost his him when I told him earlier I knew how to handle cops – boy did I get that one wrong. I had to get his trust back. We cruised into the lobby and I breezed confidently over to the receptionist.

"Good afternoon, I'm here to meet Nicholas Vargas the third." I'd chosen my debonair voice.

"Your name sir?"

"Mr. Lovejoy."

"For a while sir."

She waddled off presumably to check with Vargas. A few minutes later she returned with a handsome, suave and sophisticated looking guy I guessed in his mid-thirties. He left her and confronted me.

"Mr. Lovejoy, Nick Vargas."

We shook hands. This guy was so smooth and

polished he even looked vaguely like George Clooney.

"Is there somewhere we can have a drink and talk?"

He nodded to the receptionist and the three of us went inside the club. I gave Ricky a wink of success and he dug it. Vargas stopped at the bar. The view of Manila Bay was spectacular through the huge ceiling to floor windows.

"Can I buy you both a drink?" He said in a well-educated accent.

Ricky told me later that they call his kind mestizo in the Philippines. It's a Spanish word meaning of mixed Filipino and any foreign ancestry. I'd say Vargas had blood going back to Spanish aristocracy. He dressed classy, looked classy with manners to burn. I took a liking to him straight away – he wasn't flaunting his graces and airs or *bunging it on* as we'd call it in Australia.

Vargas smiled gracefully, "No can do, house rules, only members can buy drinks. What will it be?"

"I'll have a Harvey Wallbanger and ...?"

"Super Dry boss."

Vargas led us to a window table.

"So Mr. Lovejoy I presume this is about Kitty?"

"Sorry for the masquerade Vargas but the name is Axis Stone. I'm a PI from Australia representing the Lovejoy family. This is my associate Ricky Esposo."

Ricky shook his hand.

"I expect the cloak and dagger charade is appropriate considering the circumstances. How can I be of help?" he said casually, unaffected by my little charade.

I could see why dames would fall for this guy, he had it all, money, status, looks, savoir-faire, and as smart as a whip. Our drinks arrived. Mine with more fruit than a Carmen Miranda headdress.

"I guess they don't get asked for Wallbangers very

often round here."

"Obviously not," Vargas said chuckling at the tropical rainforest sprouting from my glass.

"Nick, mind if I call you that?" I asked.

He nodded affirmatively.

"Are you and Kitty lovers?"

"That's a touch personal, but yes."

"So how long have you two been an item?"

"I met her at Gramercy Bar the week after she opened there, so that was what ... um, eight months ago I guess."

"At that time was she seeing someone else?"

"No."

"You seem positive of that?"

"She would have told me."

"Not all dames tell the truth," I smirked.

"She's not a *dame* Mr. Stone."

By the statement I gathered he really cared for the broad.

"Do you have any idea who might have kidnapped her?"

"My best guess would be Ringo Raye."

"And why do you say that?"

"Because Raye went public saying Kitty was his girlfriend and then lost face when I came along. So I guess you could say she *was* seeing someone, but it was more like Raye was stalking her."

"Stalking her? That sounds serious."

"She wanted nothing to do with him once she learned the real nature of his business. At first she thought he was just a nightclub owner but she soon learned clubs were only a cover for his criminal activities."

"Do you think he's in the drug trade?"

"I have no reason to doubt that but no proof either."

"So she never mentioned anything about that to

you?"

"No."

"Did she find it tough to break up with him?"

"Put it this way, he's not the sort of guy who would easily accept being dumped. He has a huge ego."

"So, were there repercussions?"

"More like a state of undeclared war."

Raye was shaping up to be the villain. I downed what I could of my drink without poking my eye out with a celery stick.

"Thanks Nick ... Sorry for the third degree but we're both on the same side here."

He flicked me a business card.

"Call me if I can be of any further help, I'm very worried about Kitty."

"Sure will."

"And if you need to come to the club, just ring first and I'll arrange it," he said with a knowing smile.

"Thanks."

We left the club.

Walking through the car park I asked Ricky, "So mate, what do you think of our Nick Vargas the third?"

"He is a straight shooter, a good man to have on your side boss."

"An honest trader huh?"

"Yes, and I think he really cares about Kitty and will help if you ask him."

"Yeah, that's good to know when money talks the talk in this place. Take me to Chicki Dee's apartment."

~~~

We pulled up outside the Fort Bonifacio condo.

"Call it a day Ricky, I'll find my way home after a chat with Chicki."

"Okay boss ..."

"The next step will be to speak with Ringo Raye. Can you arrange that?"

"That might take some doing boss."

"Let's meet at 8 A.M., by the pool for breakfast again and we'll see how you got on."

"Okay boss, you got pesos for taxi?"

"Yeah, I've got a couple of thousand. That enough?"

"It should only cost two hundred and fifty pesos, it's not very far from here to the Shang ... any more and the cabbie is ripping you off."

"Cool bananas! Catch you Ricky."

I climbed out of the car and went up to the apartment intercom. Someone was coming out so I slipped inside through the open door.

You know that feeling when you know something is terribly wrong? Well, I had it in bucket loads. When I reached the apartment I found the door wide open. I pulled my gun and stealthily slipped inside. A quick scan of the living room found no sign of her.

"Chicki! Are you there?" I called out tentatively.

I checked the bedroom – nothing – then the en-suite and I found her perched naked on the toilet with her head titled back and her throat slit from ear to ear – her naked body was drenched in blood. She'd been murdered and it looked to me like it hadn't happened long ago.

"Ah Chicki, why?" I mumbled regretfully. I holstered my gun and backed out of the room, careful not to leave any footprints in the large pool of blood on the tiled floor. Suddenly I felt the prod of cold steel in my back.

"Hands in the air – real slow!"

I obeyed.

"Look, I'm a private eye. I found her like this."

Suddenly the lights went out.

Chapter Four

I woke with a massive headache in a stinking police cell. There was shit and piss all over the floor and I was laying in it. I felt a lump on the back of my head and then struggled to my feet. Just then the cell door flew open, two cops rushed in grabbed an arm each and manhandled me out up a corridor and into a brightly lit interrogation room. At least it smelt better. They dumped me in a chair.

"Your ID says Axis Stone private detective from Australia."

The cop doing the talking was in uniform with an angry head, and by the pips on his epaulettes, he had rank.

"So you can read, that's a good start. Am I being charged?" I growled, thinking that would be my best defense.

"I didn't say you could speak?"

A blow to the side of my head set my left ear ringing.

"Hey, cut the physical shit! I'll be letting my embassy know ..."

"Shut up! What were you doing at Dee's apartment?"

"Can I answer?"

"Yes, that was a question."

"She is a friend, I was visiting."

"So why did you cut her throat?"

I didn't feel comfortable being in a foreign country accused of a murder that I didn't commit – I'd seen shit like that on documentaries – how they can lock you in a cell and throw away the key.

"Take a look at me," I showed him my hands. "See any blood? Her throat was cut for Christ's sake.

Obviously I didn't kill her! What would my motive be? Anyway, how come the police arrived just after me ... a tip off? It was obviously a set up. You know that."

"That's for us to determine Stone. Lock him up."

They dragged me back to that stinking cell. An hour later I was set free without any explanation.

I was taken to the desk sergeant where I collected my wallet minus my money.

Pissed off and stinking like a bucket of prawns in the sun, I hopped a cab to the Shang. Experience had me wise enough to keep a twenty-buck note in my shoe, for an emergency so I had the cab fare.

~~~

Boy was I glad to be back in my room. I jumped into a steaming hot shower to burn off the prison stench ... and was just getting soaped up when I heard a loud knock at the door. Cursing, I quickly threw on a robe. The knocks were becoming impatient.

"All right, all right keep your shirt on."

I opened the door and two big mugs pushed their way into my room and forced me onto the bed at gunpoint.

"Hey, what the fuck's going on here?"

A sharp looking guy with a hip haircut wearing a finely tailored suit followed them in.

They set up a chair for him in front of me. Who is this dude, royalty?

"Your reputation precedes you Mr. Stone," he said with an educated accent – another mestizo like Vargas only rougher round the edges and sleazy. He reminded me of Christian Bale only with shark eyes.

"Yeah, and to whom do I owe the pleasure?"

"Ringo Raye ... pocket the hardware boys."

The thugs hid their pieces and I relaxed a little.

"Why the grand entrance Raye? You could have called first."

"I figured I had the right after paying a thousand buck bribe to bust you out of the big house."

It was obvious this guy had serious connections. I'm jailed accused of murder and he gets me out – what a system. No wonder Cortez knocked me for what I earn. I was impressed. Raye looked cunning: not a bloke to be messed with I observed. Dressed sharp in a black tailored suit, with a white T underneath, he eased back in the chair and crossed his legs like he was about to enjoy a show on TV.

"So why cut me loose?" I fired at him trying to rival his menacing vibe.

"Because I'm being fingered for a kidnapping I didn't commit, next it will be Dee's murder. I figure now you've experienced some local police hospitality, you might be amenable to co-operating, especially seeing you now owe me a big drink. "

"Listen Raye, I didn't ask to be bailed out, so let's leave it to me just tipping my hat in thanks."

"Not in my town, Stone," he growled coolly. "Now listen to me very carefully – either you work with us or against us and believe me – you don't want me as your enemy."

I got the vibe ... he wasn't just whistling Dixie.

"So who kidnapped Kitty?"

He lit a cigarette.

"No smoking on this floor Raye."

"I'm the exception. Look, there are three choices. Vargas is desperate to get me out of the way. Cortez wants me behind bars and will use Kitty as bait to get me, and low-life Nelson is going broke and would do anything to get himself out of hock. Take your fuckin' pick."

"Okay, let's start with Vargas," I said. "Who's the boyfriend, you or him?"

"Me – why else would I have made her the star

attraction at my club and then made public in the newspapers that she's my girl, huh?" He barked irritably.

"Does she feel the same way?"

He nervously twisted one of a number of rings on his fingers – a sure sign he was about to lie.

"Yeah, if Chicki had lived she would have confirmed that but someone made damn sure she wasn't going to talk, didn't they? Did you ask her about me?"

"Hmm, I guess you're right, no I didn't. What about Cortez, what's his beef with you?"

"Blames me for the murder of his brother."

"Did you kill him?"

"No. His brother was a police undercover operative, a fuckin' nark, he got whacked in a drug bust. What can I say?"

"So that leaves Nelson, what's the scoop on your relationship with him?"

"Like I said the guy is a fuckin' low life, he'd do anything to get his ass out of hock."

"Isn't that the pot calling the kettle black?"

"Watch your mouth Aussie," he growled with a stare that made the hairs on my forearms stand at attention.

I got the message – cut the wise cracks – but I couldn't resist one more.

"Then maybe Aliens abducted Kitty ... because there's been no ransom demand, and that isn't normal."

Raye fired me a long menacing stare, "I've stated my case Stone, now you get on with being a private dick. If you need some muscle to help then call me."

He handed over my smartphone the police had taken from me. "Tito, give him his piece."

The big man handed over my gun and holster. Raye stood.

"See, no dramas, it's even loaded. Now we are acquainted ... Aliens or whoever it is, I want them nailed ... I want Kitty back."

"You run the town Raye ... why don't you get her?"

"Too much heat."

He strode to the door and stopped.

"My numbers in your phone under R. Oh, there's plenty of texts from your buddy Ricky Esposo, you better let him know you're alive."

With that he and his henchmen cleared out and I immediately got Ricky on the line to fill him in.

~~~

I was tired and was about to hit the hay when there was a knock at the door. My first thought was, not again. This time I went armed but didn't need to open the door, I found a note sticking out from under it. I yanked the door open and checked up the corridor but saw no one. I went back inside sat down and read the note. I rang Ricky and read it to him.

"It says for me to go alone to the Star Bar in Quezon City at midnight tonight and ask for Zorro at the bar ... for fifty thousand pesos I will learn where Kitty Lovejoy is. What do you think Ricky?"

"I think it's what you say bulls shit."

"That's *bull* shit Ricky."

"No I mean it."

"Yeah, yeah, I know ... but why would somebody go to all the trouble of delivering me a note at the hotel if there's nothing to it?"

"That's what they want you to think. It could be anyone who knows about the case – all they want to do is to rob the foreigner."

"What time is it?" I mumbled checking the room clock. "Half of ten."

"You're not really thinking of going are you boss?"

"What are your plans for the evening?"

"I've got to drop some money to my family in Diliman."

"Is that anywhere near this Quezon City?"

"Yes, it's in Quezon City."

"So how about you drop me at the Star Bar on the way?"

~~~

I cashed a thousand US in traveler's checks at the cashier, which got me a little over fifty grand in pesos, sounded a lot. I thought, shit if I cashed all my bucks into pesos I'd be a millionaire.

I waited for Ricky to pick me up and then we headed for Quezon City. The traffic wasn't bad and forty minutes later we pulled up outside the tiny nightclub. It was just before midnight.

"You ring me and I will pick you up boss, I'm only fifteen minutes away. You sure you don't want me to come with you?"

"No, it's okay, if you don't hear from me by 1 A.M., bring the cavalry."

"I hope you didn't bring your gun."

"Not that silly Ricky," I chuckled getting out of the Corolla. If he only knew I was that silly, there was no way I was going to waltz into the Star Bar on my ace unarmed. I watched Ricky drive off and then headed for the front door that was dressed up in fairy lights like Christmas.

Disco music from the seventies was pounding ... it felt like I'd entered a time warp. A solitary mirror ball suspended from the ceiling was firing stars everywhere and they animated the half dozen couples grooving on the dance floor. A bar stretched along the back wall of the otherwise dark unembellished room – black walls, black floors – black tables and chairs – not a lot of imagination had gone into the decor. There were four or five punters seated on bar stools at the bar all of them staring in my direction. I felt by the way they were pegging me they must have thought I'd arrived from outer space. Anyhow, attention has never ruffled my feathers, so I headed for the bar. I pulled up a bar stool and waited for the barman to work up the courage to approach me. He got in front of me and then just stared at me blankly so I took the initiative.

"Give me a Jack Daniels and coke." I wasn't game to ask for a Harvey Wallbanger, not in this hole – never know what I'd get.

"Sorry sir, only beer."

I looked at all the spirit bottles decorating the shelves on the wall at back of him and pointed at a bottle of Jack.

"What's that di ba?" I thought to throw in a bit of Tagalog I'd learned to help.

He grabbed the bottle and showed it to me. It was empty. He waved his hand at the rest of them.

"All gone."

I got it ... empty was the word he needed – they were all for display.

"Okay, I'll take a San Miguel super dry."

He brought me a bottle and no glass.

"How mucho?"

"Twenty five pesos."

I slipped him a hundred pesos bill. But before he could take it I held it down on the bar top with my index finger.

"Where is Zorro?" I bargained.

He pursed his lips and pointed his chin in the direction of a door at the back. I wouldn't have made it out if it hadn't been for the mirror ball illuminating it just in time.

"Keep the change," I said generously. The tip was about a buck fifty. I took my beer and cruised over to the door. Before I knocked I looked back at the barman, he was on the phone, I guessed to Zorro. It didn't surprise me when the door suddenly jerked open without me knocking but it did surprise me who'd opened it. She was wearing a thigh-length black robe, and the way her breasts moved freely beneath it as she led the way into the dimly lit room, I figured she was wearing nothing underneath, which made the world seem a little brighter. Like I always say, there's nothing better than sex to take a man's mind off nonessentials.

"Sit down Mr. Stone," she said huskily. "I'm glad you could make it."

I sat in the armchair in front of the desk and put my bottle of beer on it. "Well let's see if coming all this way was worthwhile," I said topped up with innuendo. "Are you Zorro?"

"Yes, did you bring the money?"

I certainly wasn't expecting a dame, especially a spunky one ... I nodded in reply. There was only a desk, a couch and a chair in the small office with a single lampshade in the corner for light. She was tall for a Filipina, long shiny back hair, shapely legs, tanned skin with exotic looks. But the light cast a certain shadow on her face that made her look suspicious. She sat on the edge of the desk and lit up a cigarette.

"You smoke?" She said in a husky feminine voice.

"Socially unacceptable these days ... Look, I'm all for public relations but what have you got to tell me?"

"Are you in a hurry Mr. Stone?" She said abruptly.

I shrugged. "Not really but it's getting late and it's a long way back to Makati."

She took a long draw of her cigarette and the glow at its tip lit up her mysterious eyes. They almost squinted, "Might be best for you to sleep over," she purred.

"Anything's possible but first it's all about Kitty Lovejoy."

She got up from the edge of the desk, irreverently discarded the cigarette butt on the floor, extinguished it under her black high heeled pump and then floated behind the desk like a stripper about to start her act. She had me intrigued. More so when she pulled a gun out of the top drawer and pointed it at me.

"Put the money on the desk Mr. Stone."

Chapter Five

I was annoyed it had come to this, but deep down inside I sort of expected it. There I was with a beautiful sexy dame and my hands held up.

"The money is down the front of my pants and I need to warn you, I don't wear underwear."

"Don't be smart Mr. Stone," she said coldly.

She cruised around to the front of the desk keeping her gun trained on me and then used the barrel to flick open my jacket. After a careful look to see if I was packing, she nodded. "Reach into your pocket and get the money, no tricks Mr. Stone or you'll get yourself shot."

I believed her, so I slowly reached inside my jacket knowing my 38 was tucked in the back of my pants and pulled out the wad of notes. I handed it over to her.

"Does this mean you're only going to rob me and there is no information?"

She wasn't about to answer instead she cautiously backed behind the desk and hit a button on the desktop hands free phone module.

"You do realize of course that I wouldn't have come here without telling the cops. If I don't show up out front of here at 1 A.M., then they'll tear this place apart looking for me."

The door opened and two nasty looking goons thundered into the room. She spoke to them in Tagalog and they fastened onto one of my arms each and then lifted me bodily out of the chair.

"So much for the one night stand," I growled at her.

They manhandled me out of the club in a big hurry. Nobody in the club paid any attention. I didn't make it easy for them by walking they had to drag me.

~~~

When they got me outside they took me over to a beat up old cab and bundled me onto the back seat. Then they cramped in the back seat either side of me and concertinaed me. Out of the blue, one of them whipped out a stiletto blade and showed it to me. I got the message. My thirty-eight was burning a hole in my back pocket, but I needed to pick the right time to use it. The driver had the engine running and dropped the clutch. The old bomb cab shook and protested and then rattled off. The guy without the knife decided to thump me in the guts just for good measure.

~~~

The pain in my stomach had subsided to a dull ache from which in a couple of years I might recover. There hadn't been any conversation at all since we left the Star Bar and I was getting lonesome for the sound of a human voice.

"Listen I paid fifty thousand pesos for this ride you could at least take me to my hotel."

I copped another brutal punch in the solar plexus for my trouble. It suddenly dawned on me why they call it the solar plexus; you see stars when someone belts you there.

I was just starting to drip from the lack of air conditioning when a car screeched out of nowhere, swerved right in front and cut us off. Our driver hit the skids to avoid a crash, and we hit the curb with a jolt and stopped. Next the barrel of a gun tapped on the side window.

"Labas!" The voice behind the gun yelled. The two goons caught the intensity of the order and obeyed immediately. When the door opened I could see Ricky in the headlights of his Corolla his gun trained on the two goons.

"Dapa!" He barked.

They hit the deck flat with their arms outstretched.

Ricky leaned inside the car and said casually, "You okay boss?"

"You call that a taxi ride without air con?" I joked at the cabbie.

Ricky didn't need to threaten him the old cabbie, he was shaking like a leaf. I got out of the jalopy and climbed into the Corolla.

Ricky got in behind the wheel and we drove off.

"Thanks Ricky ... You didn't go home huh?"

"No boss, thought it best to wait outside the Star Bar for you."

"Lucky you did I think I was being taken for a one way ticket to ride."

"You mean lucky I woke up ... I was asleep. They wouldn't have killed you anyway boss, probably just stuck you with a knife and left you to bleed out in the boondocks."

"Lovely ... the lack of air con was torture enough."

"They weren't pros," he added.

"How could you tell?"

"They were shit scared."

I kicked back in the seat and yawned, "Okay let's go visit your folks."

"No way boss, first we need to get your fifty thousand back."

~~~

We pulled up outside the Star Bar.

"You said you're not armed but I think you are boss," Ricky said with a cheeky grin.

"That's what I like about you Ricky, you see right through me."

"Okay, I'm experienced with situations like this, so you leave it up to me. But have your piece ready."

"I hear you," I said getting out of the Corolla happy for Ricky to take control.

"Keep close," Ricky said before he rushed off into

the club straight up to the bar. There was no one on the dance floor and only two punters at the bar ... the same barman serving as before.

"That him?" Ricky asked me pointing at the barman.

"Yep," I replied gruffly.

Ricky pushed in-between the two punters, eyed them both with a look to kill and growled, "Vamoose!" They got the idea and high-tailed it out of the club quick smart, leaving the barman stood frozen. Ricky leaned on the bar and asked him quietly, "Where is Zorro?"

The rat-faced barman shrugged his shoulders disinterested. Ricky waved his hand to come closer so he could whisper something to him. Thinking he was about to earn himself a bribe, Rat-Face moved closer. Like lightning, Ricky grabbed his arm and then dragged him bodily up onto the bar. Rat-Face struggled and thrashed about on his back like a captured Mackerel. Ricky pounced and gripped him by the throat. The barman stopped thrashing.

"Asan siya!" Ricky said sternly.

With eyes the size of dinner plates, terrified, the barman pointed a shaky finger at the office door.

"Is that where you went before boss?"

"Sure is," I confirmed.

Ricky glared at the barman then shouted, "Umalis ka dito!" Whatever he said Rat-Face got the message ... Ricky dragged him off the bar hard so that he landed with a thump on his ass on the floor. The barman leapt to his feet and then hightailed it out of the Star Bar like a rocket.

We went up to the office door with our guns drawn and held up like a Swat team on a TV show. A nod from Ricky and I kicked the door open. We barged in with our guns held ready and stopped with me aiming at Zorro behind her desk and Ricky with his gun on a big guy seated in a chair opposite her. They both sprang to their feet shocked by our sudden invasion.

Ricky rushed the big guy and without saying a word just a sharp wave of the gun forced him to sit back down in the chair. A gun up to his head guaranteed he wasn't about to put up a fight.

"Put your hands up and get them away from the desk Zorro!" I ordered. "Where's my fucking money?"

"He's got it!" She snapped indignantly staring at the big man. "I just paid off my debt with it."

Ricky didn't muck around, he immediately pushed his thirty-eight hard against the big guys left temple and cocked the trigger.

"The money, where is it? "

"My pocket," he stammered.

"Hand it over, try anything and I'll paint the wall with your brains."

It worked. He dug into his side pocket in a flurry and then carefully, nervously, withdrew a roll of notes. Ricky snatched the roll out of his hand and threw it to me. I caught it, counted out fifty grand and threw the excess on the desk.

"There's enough left there to pay off your debt ... it's yours if you're up front with me."

Hands in the air she sighed and rolled her eyes impatiently.

"What's your real name?" I barked.

She looked at the money on the desk, then back at me, thought it over and then cautiously said while keeping a nervous eye on the big guy, "Rita Gutierrez."

"Who put you up to this? Was it him?" I hounded her.

Ricky angrily jabbed his gun even harder into the big guy's temple.

"No! No! No!" She pleaded. "It has nothing to do with him. I heard about it, did some research and figured

I could make the money I needed."

"Very enterprising of you Rita but you picked the wrong mark," I said satisfied with her story.

~~~

In the car on our way to Diliman to see Ricky's family, I asked Ricky, "Do you think she was telling the truth?"

"I don't know boss. I can't believe a woman with her looks needs to pull a stunt like that to make money, I think there's more to it than meets the eye."

"Yeah, I'm with you on that mate. Felt to me like it was a set up, a distraction, someone trying to either frighten the crap out of me or put me off the scent."

"Maybe both boss."

"I think you're right. Have you heard that name before Gutierrez?"

"It's a common name here in the Philippines."

"Well I'll just add it to my list of interest bearing grudges."

Ricky thought that was pretty funny, but to me the list was a very real.

~~~

It was only a quick visit to Ricky's family home in Diliman. A close family and small by Filipino standards, the younger brother was working in the States. In their mid-seventies both parents were not in good health. The old man had Parkinson's disease, and the Mum with osteoarthritis, but even with those terrible afflictions they were both in good spirits, happy to see their son and most welcoming to his foreigner friend. The purpose for the visit was for Ricky to drop off some money to tie them over. With me being an orphan having only Foster parents, I admired Ricky's devotion to his folks ... my estimation of had grown in leaps and bounds.

~~~

On the way back to the Shangri-La, I asked Ricky if his folks got the old age pension. He said they did but that it only amounted to three hundred pesos a month each, that's six dollars US each, and wouldn't feed a dog. I was beginning to feel for these people, to them poverty had become a way of life. A class society with a massive population consisting of the very rich, a small middle class and then the masse: or the masses ... and let me tell you it's no wonder life is so cheap because the average monthly wage is only two hundred and seventy nine dollars US. Ricky went on to tell me that six percent of the Philippine economy is owned by two ethnic Chinese business magnates with a combined net worth of nearly fourteen billion US dollars. It's no wonder this place is riddled with corruption. I don't think a history of being occupied by so many different countries over the centuries has given the people of the Philippines the time to develop individuality: a sense of self. In the beginning they were a bunch of Malay tribes that in 5 A.D., were infiltrated and then assimilated by Muslims. Then came the Chinese, who gatecrashed the party, mixed with the indigenous population and continue to do so. In 1591 they were conquered and colonized by the Spanish, then in the 16th century the British, then America in 1898 until 1933 when the Japanese kicked them out. In 1942 the USA elbowed the Japs and reoccupied the place from 1945 until 1992 when they finally withdrew their military forces – it's no wonder these poor people have an identity crisis, they haven't a clue who they are.

Changing the subject Ricky asked me, "You seemed attracted to Zorro boss."

"Yeah, I don't know Ricky, there's just something about a hot babe with a gun in her hand that gets my juices flowing,"

"That could be a dangerous habit," he said flatly.

"You hit the nail on the head there, buddy boy. Women have been the bane of my existence ever since

I can remember – comes with not having a real mother I reckon," I admitted.

"Do you lose it when you get horny?"

"Put it this way one whiff of those female pheromones and rational thinking goes right out the window."

"I'll try and remember that in future," he chuckled.

"You saying I stuffed up with Zorro?"

"Just an observation boss."

"Tell me more."

"You were armed but yet you allowed her to take control of you. Could have got yourself killed."

"I hear you ... I hear you."

The truth always hurts and more so when someone you hardly even know gets a bead on you. My one fatal flaw had been on show again and I had been lucky to escape in one piece – fuck, when will I ever learn? Sounds like a Pete Seeger song.

By the time Ricky threw me out at the Shang it was nearly 3 A.M. We agreed to meet by the pool at eight in the morning. I dragged myself up to my room and fell into the sack still dressed.

Chapter Six

I was busy taking in some of the crumpet on show in and around the Shang pool when Ricky rolled up.

"Morning boss."

"Park your bod Ricky, what's up?" I asked.

"Word is out on the street the cops are gunning for you."

"Why's that?"

"Cortez wasn't told about your arrest or release until after the fact. I think he knows who bailed you out."

"Yeah?" I glanced at him over my Raybans. "Well if Raye's word is gospel, then Cortez would think I've pitched in with the guy he suspects of murdering his brother. It makes perfect sense he'd come after me. Someone murdered Chicki, and then called the cops to set me up. The question begs: how did Raye know I'd been arrested?"

"You suspect him?"

"Right now everybody is a suspect except you and I, and even thou art a little dubious."

"What do you mean boss?"

"Nothing, it was just a joke."

My phone vibrated. I flashed Ricky the caller ID: Lola Lovejoy. He nodded. I stood up, took the call and talked while pacing up and down poolside.

"Hey Lola what's up? You have? What! So it was a guy ... any accent? No, right ... did you speak to Kitty? Hmm, okay ... you what? ... In the background? Yeah that might mean something. No don't do anything, let me mull it over and I'll get back to you. I'm making a little headway here. It won't be long before we get a break. Okay bye."

I hung up and returned to Ricky, "Big news, there's

been a ransom demand. A guy with a disguised voice phoned the Lovejoy's and asked for two million US to be digitally transferred to a numbered bank account within forty-eight hours. He threatened to cut off one of Kitty fingers each day until he gets the money."

"Did she ...?"

"Yeah, she spoke to Kitty, she's all right."

In the old days ransom was paid with bags of cash: notes were traceable by numbers, dye or later GPS homing microdots on individual bills. Now it's a digital transfer to a numbered account and impossible to trace. Technology took the edge the good guys had and gave it to the crooks. I sat back down deep in thought.

"What are you thinking boss?"

"Lola said she could hear lapping water and birds in the background. What does that tell you?"

"A boat, the beach, a lake ... a resort hotel."

"I'll need a safe-house Ricky, can you arrange one? No, better still, here," I handed him my phone. "Ring Cortez, I should confront him before this gets out of hand."

Ricky spoke Tagalog to the police operator, while I paced about weighing up options. The question of who killed Chicki and why, bothered me. Now that the kidnapping was about money, the plot had thickened. The question was – which suspect needs that much dough and knows the family well enough to be confident of getting it? Who has the readies and the savvy to set up an offshore numbered bank account? You'd think that would eliminate Cortez, leaving Nelson, Raye and Vargas. Would Vargas need money? I don't think so he's already loaded. My bet was on Nelson, though Raye is such a cunning operator he couldn't be discounted. Which one of them knew I would visit Chicki?

"Boss, Cortez will meet you."

The rendezvous was set for Café Breton in the outdoor plaza section of Greenbelt: a large modern shopping mall in Makati not far from the Shangri-La Hotel.

~~~

We found Cortez under an umbrella at a table in the alfresco section of the popular café.

"Stone, I selected a neutral location as a sign of good faith."

"I'm impressed," I said pulling up a seat opposite him, as did Ricky.

It was lunchtime. I checked the menu.

"The Excalibur looks good. You eating Cortez?"

"You paying?" He asked.

"Yeah." I passed him the menu.

"What were you doing at Dee's apartment?" he questioned nonchalantly while studying the menu.

"Getting her to talk about the kidnapping," I returned serve.

He lowered the menu and eyeballed me. "Did you kill her?"

"Now that would have been pretty stupid of me wouldn't it? No, don't be ridiculous."

He handed the menu to Ricky.

"That's what I thought. So who set you up then?" Cortez asked coldly. "And who bailed you out and why?"

I was pondering whether to tell him about the ransom demand.

"I'll tell you what, let's exchange some home truths – agree?"

The waiter arrived.

"I'll have an Excalibur and an iced coffee – how about you Cortez?"

"A Neptune and a short black."

Ricky added, "Make that two."

"Okay Stone, what have you got?"

The passing parade of sexy ladies was distracting for me but I managed to make a decision on what to focus on.

"Firstly yes, Raye bailed me out but you know that don't you – I have no idea why or how he even knew I'd been arrested. Secondly, there has been a ransom demand."

"When?"

"This morning ... Two million US to a numbered bank account within forty-eight hours."

"That changes everything. All right Stone, now that there has been a demand we will need to be on the same page. I will come clean with you. You were not set up by the police, someone dialed 117, and it's true, I have been after Raye for murdering my brother – that might have clouded my judgment until now, but I'll put it aside now. Vargas, Raye and Nelson are my three main suspects but there is a fourth."

The food arrived momentarily distracting us.

"A fourth you say?"

"Yes, the fiancé of Nick Vargas ... Bianca Gutierrez: a socialite gold digger who didn't enjoy for being dumped by him for Kitty Lovejoy."

Bells were ringing for Ricky and myself. We exchanged a quizzical expression.

"I see the name means something to both of you," Cortez said solemnly.

"We had a bit of a run in last night with one Rita Gutierrez alias Zorro."

"Ha!" Cortez grunted. "That cheap hustler ... she's a relative, runs a cheap bar in Quezon City."

"The Star Bar," Ricky said.

""Yes that's the one. Did she try and blackmail you or something?"

"You could say that," I said.

"That's her form," Cortez chuckled.

"So what about this Bianca Gutierrez, is she made of the same stuff?" I probed.

"A class act but still with a bad streak," he said.

"Runs in the family," Ricky scoffed.

"Why's that?" I asked.

"She was probably the meal ticket to her family," Ricky chimed in. "Their one big chance to get into the elite old-money set through Vargas."

"Wouldn't be the first time a spurned jealous lover took revenge in this town," Cortez observed chewing his sandwich.

"Why the ransom?" I posed.

"Money is everything in Manila," Cortez admitted, "and they would have the means to set it up."

"By *they* you mean the Gutierrez family?" I questioned.

Cortez was growing on me ... he'd dropped the arrogance and lightened up.

"They would stop at nothing to get rich," he chuckled.

For the first time I noticed his gold front tooth, made him look even more like Tuco.

"Ricky, I'd better meet with this Bianca Gutierrez."

"I'll set it up boss."

"So how did it turn out with Zorro? From memory she is quite a dish," Cortez smirked.

"Let's just say I'm putting it down to experience," I said smugly.

"A close encounter of the Filipina kind, there will be more of those before you are through here Mr. Stone, just make sure you count your fingers after you've dabbled."

Over lunch we resolved to keep on the same page. Cortez would focus on Dee's murder while I would continue to interview suspects. Sooner or later we expected a break in the case – but the clock was ticking.

~~~

Ricky dropped me at the Shang and after some research I made a conference call to the Lovejoy's.

"Lola, Winston?"

"Hi there Stone, we're feeling a little more confident after the ransom demand, at least we now know where we stand," Winston admitted gruffly.

"True. I checked the bank account, it's a hole in the wall bank in St. Vincent, West Indies, impossible to access."

"Can we put someone there to watch for a withdrawal?"

"No Winston, from there the money will almost certainly be automatically transferred to another bank and then another, until it's eventually collected from goodness knows where."

"So what should we do then?" Lola asked, emotionally.

"Locate her inside the time limit," I suggested tentatively.

"And if we fail?" She questioned.

"Then she loses a digit. Look, the kidnapper wants money, he's not going to harm her, it would mean dealing with a hysterical hostage and managing a nasty wound – and that's just not on."

"Are you suggesting we call his bluff?" Winston snapped.

"Oh please give us a better alternative than that?" Lola pleaded.

"Okay, pay the two mill, get her back, then with her help, we'll track down the kidnapper. That's my advice," I said unyieldingly.

It was no surprise when they chose the payout option, and that translated to a totally different approach from our end. The hand-over would be tough with no assurances that once he's got the money the kidnapper will surrender the hostage – he might simply ask for more. We needed to make a counterproposal to prevent that from happening, but without direct contact with the kidnapper, we'd have to wait for his next call and that meant possibly missing the deadline and risking Kitty losing a digit. I phoned Cortez.

"I've spoken with the Lovejoy's, and they're willing to pay up. Yes, no assurances. We could go to the press with a counter offer to attract the kidnapper's attention? Say – *Ransom demand made for Kitty Lovejoy – family will pay but first need release assurance.* Good, I'll leave it up to you to run it? Next we need to devise a release and arrest strategy. Okay, my hotel room 0900 hours tomorrow." I hung up and immediately got a call.

"Stone speaking ... Ringo what's up? Tonight out front of the Shangri-La at ten. What's this about? Okay, done."

Raye had something to tell me in person, cloak and dagger stuff I know but that's how it was going to be played from now on. I was thinking about hitting the swimming pool to get a taste of the fluff available at the hotel when Ricky rang. He'd set up a meeting with Bianca Gutierrez at Café Havana in Greenbelt. I knew where it was, next door to Café Breton where we had lunch with Cortez ... we agreed to meet there at 6 P.M. I decided to use the spare time for some research on the net.

It was only a short walk from the Shang to Café Havana, but at that time of day the footpaths were so crowded, I ran late. Fortunately Ricky had got there early and grabbed a table in the alfresco section.

Café Havana is more a bar than a café. It offers small Spanish Tapas dishes and an extensive drinks menu. A popular happy hour hang it was my kind of joint.

Gutierrez hadn't arrived, so I ordered our drinks.

"Raye phoned, wants to meet tonight," I told Ricky.

"Why"?"

"He wouldn't say over the phone, he'll pick me up at ten."

"You might need me along boss?"

"Nar, I'll be okay, either he's trying to bond with me to get some dirt on a suspect or he's planning to take me for a ride."

Shaking his head Ricky said, "Boss you can't trust anyone in this town, especially you ... a foreigner! They'll knock you over just like that!" He clicked his fingers.

The click rang home – life could be snuffed out just that easily here. I must admit, after what happened to Chicki and my time in that stinking cell along with the Star Bar treatment, I was inclined to take heed of his warning. I don't think of myself a slow learner but something was telling me I needed to meet with Raye.

The drinks arrived and compared to my last Wallbanger at the Yacht Club, this one had had a haircut – far less vegetation – but it did have one of those little umbrellas that I quickly flicked. The place was filling up fast and the scenery first class. Lots of long suntanned legs and plunging necklines – and the girls look sexy as well – only joking.

Ricky's phone rang. I looked up and sighted the most gorgeous babe I'd seen since meeting Lola and Zorro heading right our way. On the phone she waved at Ricky. Wow! Kitty must be something special for Vargas to have dropped this stunner, I figured. I stood to greet her.

Chapter Seven

"**M**iss Gutierrez, I'm Axis Stone. Please sit," I gestured.

She sat and daintily crossed her long shapely, suntanned legs. At five eight she was tall for a Filipina and though a better sort than Zorro, there were similarities. Wearing a designer white satin blouse with a plunging neckline that had my imagination screaming for more – a sleek light brown knee-length skirt, she reeked high-maintenance. I recognized the bag on her arm as a Gadino, retails for around forty grand US – then there'd be little change from a grand for her beige Christian Louboutin high-heels sandals. Tasteful accessories: a Cartier Crash watch, no rings – a pair of diamond stud earrings: a carat a-piece, Carven sunglasses – and her shiny long black hair worn up which showed off her jaw line and lovely neck to perfection. I'd learned to read threads and accessories from my mentor DI Malone of CID Sydney, he taught me they were the best window into the personality of any male or female.

"You want to ask me about Nicholas? I was in the area so agreed to meet you, otherwise I wouldn't have bothered." She snarled arrogantly with pouted red painted lips.

Boy, this bird had the temper of a rabid dog. She'd be amazing in bed. Made me wonder if she just had a distaste of foreigners or if she was just a genuine twenty-five year old Gen-Y snob.

"I'm glad you bothered coming, you've brightened up my day," I said with my best smile that generally works to lighten things up.

"Well, I'll be, a gentleman – guys like you are a

rarity these days," she quipped and crossed her long shapely naked legs. She caught me checking them out and by her facial expression, liked it.

"Well, thank you Miss Gutierrez, may I call you Bianca?"

"No! My friends call me Bee."

The ice had broken – maybe because she picked up that I fancied her.

"So Bee, did Ricky mention what I do?"

"You're an Aussie private *dick* retained by the family of the red witch."

I wasn't sure why she emphasized dick and it made me wonder.

"You mean Kitty?"

"Call her what you like but red witch is a more accurate description of the bitch."

There was obviously no love lost between them.

"Do you have any idea who might have kidnapped her?"

"No, but they get a standing ovation from me."

"I see ... so tell me what happened when Vargas broke up with you?" I asked ignoring her angst.

"Now that one will cost you a drink."

"Certainly, I'm sorry ... what will it be?"

She lowered her sunnies and peered over the top of them with a dreamy squint, "A glass of French champagne of course."

This broad would be more expensive to run than a Bugatti Veyron, and I know which I'd prefer, though she sure has bedroom eyes.

Ricky signaled a waiter and ordered.

"It was my idea to see the red witch at Gramercy. Our friends had seen her perform and were impressed. We, that's Nick and I, had been an item for a year and were planning on getting married mid next year. He'd met Ringo Raye at a casino, I expect you know all about him? He was the red witch's lover — it was all over the social pages."

Bee Gutierrez wasn't about to pour her heart out, she was way too tough-a-broad for that.

"Raye brought the witch over to our table after her set."

"Why?"

"To show her off I guess, he's like that. Seems Nick was more impressed with her than I thought because two weeks later he told me it was over between us."

"Didn't give you a reason?"

"He just said he'd realized marriage wasn't right for him now. I of course said fine, let's just wait. But he said he needed a break from our relationship and was planning a trip to the States ... to think. Later I found out he wasn't going there to think alone."

"Kitty?"

"You got it in one ... my, aren't we smart? Now where's that Goddamned drink!" She barked like a spoilt brat.

Suddenly her Gadino handbag started playing *Shake it Off* by Taylor Swift. She whipped out her phone and checked the caller ID.

"I need to take this," she said curtly.

She got up and walked around behind me to take the call. Within seconds she was shouting at the phone in Tagalog. I couldn't understand what she was saying, so I whispered surreptitiously to Ricky.

"Who is she arguing with?"

"Her brother."

"What's it about?"

"Sounds like he doesn't approve of her being here."

Her voice was full of raw emotion. Suddenly the argument stopped — she returned and flopped into her seat, fuming. Her demeanor had reshaped to accommodate her petulance. I sensed she was about to cut out – but I needed more answers and was saved by the late arrival of her flute of champagne. After a sip she calmed down.

"I'm sorry ... that was my brother Arnel."

"That's okay, is everything all right? ... You look ..."

"Sometimes he comes on too strong with the big brother shit," she growled.

By the intensity of the argument it seemed more than that to me but I let it go. Her skirt has ridden up over her knee and I thought I could see a little cleave like she wasn't wearing panties. She caught me looking and crossed her legs.

"So, did Nick go to the States with Kitty?" I asked her.

"No, but it didn't end there. My parents wouldn't accept that after they'd given Nick permission to marry me he'd renounced it, so they took it up with his family and the Church," she said with a catty expression that wasn't becoming at all.

Before she could utter another word, just as she was taking a sip of champagne, someone pushed through the crowd and smacked the flute right out of her hand. It shattered on the pavement. I jumped up. The assailant grabbed Bee by the arm and tried to forcibly drag her away from our table – both of them screaming in Tagalog.

I grabbed the guy by the shoulder and shouted, "Hey fella, let her go!"

He took a swipe at me ... I saw it coming, swayed and his fist grazed my chin. Instinctively, I returned serve with a right jab that I landed right on the button. He went down like a bag of potatoes. You'd think Bianca would appreciate being rescued but no, she turned on me and let fire with both barrels.

"You've killed my brother you fucking monster!" She screamed hysterically.

A flurry of punches followed that were more threatening that her brother's. Fortunately Ricky came to the rescue, grabbed both her arms from behind and growled at her in Tagalog to calm down. I checked her brother. He wasn't knocked out, only dazed with a bleeding nose and a cut lip.

Two security guards appeared out of the crowd and helped him up. He was a good-looking guy, even with a bloody face. A mestizo: half Spanish and Filipino, shorter than me, under 6 feet, early thirties, wiry but a cut build, dressed in designer jeans and a polo shirt.

A guard stood between us to keep the peace.

"Come on Bianca, let's go!" He growled angrily trying to pull away from the guard's grip.

"That's no way to treat your sister!" I hollered at him.

Still restrained by the guard, Arnel got in my face.

"Stay away foreigner or you'll wind up in a freakin' body-bag!"

Constraining Bianca, Ricky chimed in. "Watch your mouth Gutierrez!"

"Let go of me!" Bianca shouted, then pulled away from Ricky and hit him with a brutal verbal spray in Tagalog. By the look on Ricky's face it wasn't very lady-like. With her anger vented, she grabbed Arnel by the arm and dragged him off into the passing throng. The guard let me go and I sat back down at the table.

"What did she say to you Ricky?"

"Ah just a childish threat boss."

"Nothing's childish my friend, I rate those two high on the suspect list, capable of anything. If my instincts are correct, then this isn't the end of it: he'll retaliate. Dig up what you can on him. I've got a gut feeling about him – crap seems to run in their family."

"You think he's the kidnapper?"

"No but he stinks of an involvement."

"Are you all right boss?"

"Yeah Ricky, he only grazed me. Anyhow, let's check the menu, I'll buy you dinner mate."

Ricky studied it.

"I should take you for Sisig, boss."

"Yeah, what's Sisig?"

"Filipino delicacy."

"If there's no rotten fish or offal in it, then I'm up for giving it a try."

Ricky laughed.

"No worries boss, nothing rotten and no guts."

~~~

We walked through Ayala Center, which was packed with a plethora of people and loads of pretty ladies and all very pleasing on the eye. We got to Glorietta 5, made our way of to the 2nd floor and entered Gerry's Grill. Ricky managed to get us a table even though the restaurant was full.

I sank into a wicker chair and studied the menu.

"I order for you, Filipino delicacies," Ricky said with a cheeky grin on his face.

- The waitress arrived and he babbled to her in Tagalog, so I had no idea what he was ordering until he got to the drinks, and then I recognized the words super dry. The appetizers arrived quickly one sizzling and smelling great the other a little suspect.

"Try this first," Ricky said pointing at the sizzling dish.

I tried it and it tasted fine.

"You like it?"

"Yeah, it's all right," I said as the beers arrived.

"Okay, try this one."

As I raised the spoon with what looked like little fish on it to my mouth I smelt something putrid ... it tasted how it smelt, gross.

"Ew!" I shrieked gagging on it. I quickly threw

down half a bottle of beer to kill the taste. "Man that is wrong, what the stuff is it?"

"Green mango with Bagoong ... fermented fish."

"Man I said nothing rotten ... you can leave me out of that one mate. What's the other one?"

"Sizzling Balut with Tofu."

"So what's Balut?" I asked hesitantly.

"Sure you can handle it? You ate it."

"Oh no, don't tell me I just ate something rancid?"

"Duckling fetus," he mumbled tentatively.

"Hmm, well I can just about handle that."

"We normally drink it down raw while it's still inside the egg."

I took another big swig of beer to wash it all down. Three more dishes arrived. The first two didn't look too offensive but the third looked like shriveled up spiders.

"What the stuff is that?" I exclaimed.

"Crunchy squid heads," Ricky said with a big smile. He picked up a couple and chewed them up. "Hmm, very good ... come on, try boss."

I wasn't going to be outdone and scooped up a bunch of them, bravely shoved them in my mouth and munched them up. I stopped chewing with a frozen look of terror and watched Ricky sink in his chair, then I relaxed my face into a smile and happily announced, "Excellent!"

Relief broke on Ricky's face. The other two dishes were sizzling pork sisig and sizzling seafood gambas, both culinary triumphs. I wasn't sold on the Bagoong or the Balut, but the other dishes were exceptional. A check arrived for one thousand and twenty pesos: ten dollars US each – unbelievably cheap. Ricky was stoked that I enjoyed some of his countries traditional dishes and I was happy to add them to my culinary database.

~~~

When I got back to the Shang, it was almost time

to meet Ringo, so I waited in the lobby. Seems that at ten on a Friday night there's a change of guard in Makati. The day-trippers clock off to bed and the night prowlers surface to strut their stuff. A row of international clocks along the wall backing reception all said it was time to be picked up, so I wandered out onto the forecourt. Filipinos are not noted for their punctuality due to the malignant traffic congestion, well that was the excuse anyway, but Ringo's mob seemed to be the exception to the rule. I recognized one of his goons through the open driver's side window of a black Pajero, and walked over to it. Seems everyone in Manila with bucks has a black Pajero.

"Tito, where's Ringo?" I asked.

"Get in. I take you to him," he said gruffly.

I climbed into the passenger seat mindful of my gun – ready in case it was another set up. Two henchmen were perched on the back seat like a pair of gargoyles.

"Where are we going?" I asked Tito. I asked Tito. I'd last met him in my room with Raye.

"One of the bosses clubs in Burgos Street."

Ah, the infamous P. Burgos Street – wall-to-wall girlie bars – the red light district of Makati. I'd not been there but I'd heard plenty about it.

Chapter Eight

When you visit a city, if you're a bloke, you quickly learn about the red light district by default, I guess. It was no surprise to learn Ringo was a stakeholder in the local sex industry.

Tito pulled the Pajero up outside a white two-story building with a flashing neon sign that said it was Foxy's. I climbed out. A large overweight doorman opened the door and while Tito parked the Pajero, the two gargoyles led me inside. The music was pumping loud and the lighting, seductive. The gargoyles pointed upstairs so I headed up the narrow dimly lit staircase. A couple of scantily dressed girls were on their way down and giggled past me. I must admit, the scallywag came out in me and I purposely faced them so that they had to squeeze past and brush my chest with their boobs.

An older woman in a black suit with long pants met me at the top of the stairs and introduced herself.

"Mr. Stone, I am Mimi, mama-san of Foxy's, please follow me."

She led me past a sushi bar and into a private room. I was immediately struck by the view through the floor to ceiling windows down to the stage below – upon which half a dozen near naked girls were slow dancing – I was impressed – a sex palace was right up my street. A single ceiling light illuminated in back of me and I turned to find Ringo seated under it in an armchair looking like an emperor.

"Axis, glad you could make it ... welcome to my club, please sit down, make yourself comfortable."

Mimi closed the door behind her and I flopped into a big comfy black leather armchair that was against the wall to the side of Ringo.

"What do you drink? You probably need one after your run-in with Arnel Gutierrez this afternoon."

"Is there anything you don't know Ringo?"

"Yeah, who's got my girl!" His eyes had an icy deadpan look that I didn't trust.

"Wish I could answer that for you, but so far my money's on Gutierrez. A Harvey Wallbanger, stirred not shaken, no vegetation."

Ringo pressed a button on the arm of his chair and the door opened to Mimi.

"A bald Wallbanger for Mr. Stone and the usual for me."

With the drinks ordered, he turned his attention back to Gutierrez.

"Why do you suspect him?"

"Avarice, that's enough to motivate any gold-digger," I said soberly.

"I don't know that he's got the guts or the brains to pull off something like that."

"So you know him then?" I probed.

"Yeah, he was hanging around the Gramercy like a bad smell. I had to move him on. "

"So, why bring me here and not to Gramercy?" I carefully changed the subject.

"To show you how the other half lives."

"Didn't realize we were so divided. Besides, I've already had brief encounter with the other half at the Star Bar?"

"Ha, Rita Gutierrez, funny."

"Yeah, AKA Zorro ... so what's funny?"

"Seems you've got problems with the entire Gutierrez family, better ask your buddy Vargas how to deal with it, he's had plenty of experience."

"So I've heard."

"Was Cortez pleased with me bailing you out?"

"Yeah, like a hole in the head ... I was thinking you only did it just to piss him off."

"Maybe so, but let me get one thing straight with you Stone, the law is crooked here – everything is crooked here ... business is done by extortion ... it's a way of life, a hangover a psychologist would say from our rebellious colonial days."

"Seems that's a common legacy for former Spanish colonies such as Mexico and most of central and South America."

"That's what you get when there's little separation between Church and state," he said assertively.

"You can hardly complain, it makes for good business for a bloke like you. I guess once you've got power and some money you can stand over most anyone, and when you can't you just buy them."

"You're a fast learner Stone."

"I like to think so," I said facetiously.

Our drinks arrived and two things impressed me – first, my Wallbanger was dressed up like it should be; and two, the bird serving them was to die for. Ringo caught me gawking at her exquisite body.

"Tina, sit with Mr. Stone."

She sat beside me, and that immediately put the brakes on our conversation. A petite girl with lovely breasts and an hourglass figure, her fluttering eyelashes did my head in.

"What do you want to know Ringo?" I asked.

"Newspapers say there's been a ransom demand. Has someone spoken to the kidnapper?"

"Yeah, he wants two mill US, and that's thrown a different light on the case."

"I would have thought it throws a bad light on Gutierrez and Nelson."

"Isn't your money on Vargas?" I questioned.

"He doesn't need the fuckin' money," he growled.

"Did you bring me here to get laid?"

"Yes."

Raye stood. "I'll be downstairs," he smiled devilishly. "Come down after you've popped your cork."

Tina got the message and as soon as he left, made a move. Her bra came off, she wriggled out of her bikini bottoms and posed ... petite, brown skinned with cute small breasts and erect nipples – I could tell she wanted me. It was sure shaping up to be a memorable night.

Tina knelt down on the carpet, slotted in between my legs and then undid my pants. Her warm mouth closed around Mr. Happy, he heard the call of the wild and instantly sprang in action.

An hour later, I wandered downstairs to find Ringo. He turned to face me from the bar and his three henchmen.

"I was going to send you another Wallbanger, but figured the banger you had was good enough."

"You're not wrong, I've got to say Filipinas have a special talent."

"We turned an obsession into an industry," he said smugly.

He led me away from the others to a dark alcove to talk in private.

"Want something to eat? We've got some nice Filipino appetizers or there's sushi?"

"No thanks already tried Bagoong and Balut and I can't say I'll be backing up for seconds."

We sat in the darkness and I looked about. There were guys with bargirls secreted away in a dozen or so little curtained alcoves around the perimeter of the room and a cavalcade of waitresses serving them. I had a good view of the stage that was elevated four feet off the floor. On it eight scantily clad girls line-danced real slow, to save energy I guess. The music tempo was such that it should've had them leaping about all over the shop. The half dozen tables directly in front of the stage and along the small catwalk were packed with punters. With their eye level up from the dancer's feet there was plenty of eye candy for them. All of the customers were Caucasian except for a group of four Japanese or Korean's in suits. They had the most girls hanging off them and were carrying on like big spenders. I guess with the sort of company expense accounts they had they were high rollers, compared to the others at any rate.

"How does it work then?" I asked Ringo.

"What the bar game?"

"Yeah."

"The girls make their money from the drinks customers buy them."

"How can they do that without getting plastered?"

"Their drinks are only shot glasses of orange juice ... they cost the punter six bucks a pop, split fifty-fifty between the house and the girl. It's all on a tab that gets reckoned up when the customer pays his bill."

"It there any hanky-panky?"

"That's up to the girl. The mama-san provides the girls ... I provide the club and the booze."

"Like you own the venue and mama puts on the gigs?"

"Something like that."

"So what happens when a punter wants to take a girl back to his hotel for a bang?"

"He pays the club a bar-fine. We get twenty percent of it for losing the girl, mama-san gets a cut ... the girl gets the rest. If she performs well she'll most probably get a tip, which she keeps."

"How much is a bar fine?"

"Depends on the club but here four thousand pesos or eighty bucks."

"Not much ... how many girls here can go out?"

"All of one hundred and fifty of them ... see the fat one on stage?"

At the end of the line of dancers wobbled a very tubby girl with big breasts and thunder thighs. Not my bag at all.

"Yep, can hardly miss her."

"She's our biggest earner."

"You've got to be kidding me!"

"There's something for everyone here, it's my policy," he said with a proud chuckle.

"Why have the mama-san?"

"She takes the heat off. I can't be busted for selling whores while she's their manager ... what they do is her business. Anyhow, enough of my business what's with your business – what's the scoop on the ransom? Does that mean Cortez will lay off my ass for a while?"

"Your nemesis – yep, I'd say so. Look, I'll tell you ... when the Lovejoy's spoke to Kitty, they heard lapping water and seabirds in the background. What does that say to you?"

"She's on a boat somewhere, so what is this a quiz?" He said soberly.

"So, who out of the possible contenders has a boat?"

"I do. Vargas. I don't know about Nelson, but he and Gutierrez would probably know someone that does."

"Where's your boat?" I asked.

"Subic Bay Yacht Club."

"And Vargas?"

"Manila Yacht Club I'd say. So?"

"First, I need to search each of the suspect's boats including yours, at the same time find out if there are others."

I still wasn't sold on Ringo. There were only two possibilities for him buttering me up and playing the good guy; either he's head over heels for Kitty and wants her back or he's the kidnapper.

"I don't get it," I mused.

"You don't fuckin' get what?" He asked angrily.

"You've got enough muscle to find the kidnapper, why are you relying on me?"

"Thought that was obvious – I don't have a pipeline to the kidnapper. Whoever he is he knows what I'm capable of. No, this has been carefully planned, this fuckin' guy is smart, he's managed to cut me and the cops out of it by directly contacting the Lovejoy's."

It was a valid point.

"All right," I said standing to leave. "I need some shut-eye."

"Want me to send Tina to your hotel room? A freebie."

"No, I've had enough pouch to last me a couple of days thanks. One last question – who killed Chicki Dee?"

"If you're asking did I do it and set you up just bust you out of jail – no. You've got to remember you're a fuckin' foreigner – word gets out on your movements. That makes you an easy mark. Whoever killed Dee wanted to shut her up. Just call me if you need Tina, or even a couple of Tina's," he sniggered like a dirty old man.

"Good to know ... but for now I need to get onto Vargas' boat."

"What about Nelson and Gutierrez?" He asked.

"I'll get my associate Ricky to check into them."

"Ricky?"

"Ricky Esposo."

"He's an ex-cop. I know of him. Tell him to watch his back."

He signaled for Tito to take me home. On the way there I thought to myself, here I am, I've only been in

Manila five minutes and I'm rubbing shoulders with the biggest crook in town, getting chauffeur driven and my best mate is a millionaire. I love this gig.

~~~

I'd just opened the door to my hotel room while checking my phone when I found a text message from Ricky I'd missed. He had news on Gutierrez and wanted me to call him ASAP. I sat on the edge of the bed and dialed him.

"Ricky, yeah, sorry its late there was too much noise at the club I didn't hear my phone ring. He owns a girlie bar called Foxy's ... Yes, my first time at one, yep, it was certainly an experience. So, what's new? You're kidding me! Okay, meet me poolside at 9 A.M."

I hit the sack.

Chapter Nine

It was identical weather to the day before. I was downing my second coffee by the pool taking in the view waiting for Ricky, when he rolled up.

"Hey, morning boss."

"Ricky, I just drank the coffee I ordered you."

"Sorry I'm late ... traffic."

I signaled a waiter for another coffee.

"So our boy has form then?" I said.

"More than that," Ricky said pulling up a chair. "Arnel Gutierrez was arrested at the same bust the brother of Cortez was murdered."

"That's a bit too much of a coincidence isn't it? Hey, check out the body on that chick getting in the pool."

"Mind on the job boss ... and just like you, Arnel Gutierrez was held only for a few hours ... then released ... no charge."

"Hmm, sounds familiar ... very suspicious. Anything else?"

I couldn't take my eyes off the beautiful buxom brunette posing at the edge of the pool. But the sudden arrival of her guy put an end to the fantasy.

"After that he tried his hand at business and went broke. You'll never guess who his investors were?"

"You've got me there."

She was looking my way and we locked eyes.

"Bugs Bunny and Daffy duck," Ricky snarled.

"Dead set," I said vaguely.

Ricky got up.

"Maybe I'll go away and come back when your big head takes control over your little head boss."

That snapped me out of my sexual haze.

"I'm sorry Ricky ... please, sit down ... I don't know

what's the matter with me … this town makes me horny as hell," I said apologetically. "Where were we?"

"You were going to guess the identity of the two investors with Arnel Gutierrez," he said sitting down.

"I've got no idea," I said paying attention.

"Nick Vargas and Raymundo Gutierrez."

"Vargas! Raymundo, who's that his father?"

"Yes. "

"I'll be damned. Did he go broke as well?"

"You bet he did, big time."

"What sort of business was it?" I asked.

"A bar."

"Why am I not surprised? Next you'll be telling me it was the Star Bar. When did all this all happen?"

"Six months ago."

"How convenient."

The bankruptcy provided motive to back my suspicion of the Gutierrez family as the kidnappers, but we needed more compelling evidence before going to Cortez with it, besides, I found the connection between Gutierrez and Cortez dubious and disturbing to say the least.

"To recap, the Lovejoy's said they heard birds and lapping water in the background when they spoke to Kitty … chances are she's being held on a boat. Raye said Vargas has a boat moored at the Manila Yacht Club, we need to check it out. We also need to find out if Nelson and the Gutierrez's have boats or friends with boats and if they do, where they are moored."

"I think Raye has a boat," Ricky said.

"Yeah he mentioned it, in place called Subic Bay. We'll check it out as well."

"We can't just go boarding boats without permission boss, they have armed guards."

"Yeah, I suppose you're right. Let me worry about that, you get on with finding out the other stuff."

While Ricky phoned around I took a quick dip in the pool so I could get a closer look at the brunette. The swim was good but the brunette was a waste of time, her looks deteriorated the closer I got. By the time I got real close I realized she was old enough to be my mother. By the time I got out of the pool, Ricky already had results.

"Boss, Nick Vargas sailed for Puerto Galera yesterday. Nelson owns a share in a boat. No news on Gutierrez yet."

"Puerto Galera, where's that?" I said toweling myself down.

"An island down south near Batangus."

"I see, where's Nelson's boat moored?

"Subic Bay Yacht Club – same as Raye."

"How far is that?"

"Two hours' drive, north."

"Let's do it."

Ricky phoned ahead and used his considerable influence to get us two rooms at the Subic Bay Yacht Club.

~~~

I enjoyed the drive there, a chance to see the countryside and it was interesting to see Mount Pinatubo looming in the distance as we drove into Olongapo. I remembered the devastating photographs of the volcano blowing its top back in 1991 and the destruction it caused.

"It says on this map that's the Mount Pinatubo that blew up?" I questioned Ricky.

"Yes boss, sure is. You know there is a conspiracy theory that the American's dropped a small bomb in the volcano to set off the eruption."

"You've got to be kidding, why would they wanna do that?"

"Because they needed an excuse to move the

military bases out of Subic Bay and Clarke Airbase, it was costing the US government a fortune and the bases had gone past their use-by-date."

"Why not just announce it?"

"There were too many Filipino jobs dependent on the bases, plus the government here wanted to keep the US military protection and the masses of money they paid each year to lease the massive complex."

"Yeah well that makes sense, but to cause such a devastating eruption – where's the proof?"

"Seismologists had been monitoring the mountain and it wasn't showing any signs of a coming eruption, it had been dormant for four hundred years. The native Aeta people living on the mountain say the birds and animals had not shown any worrying signs and they're generally the first indication of an eruption about to occur. Then they heard an explosion inside the mountain the day before the eruption. Apparently, seismologists were able tell the difference on their eruption monitoring equipment between a natural explosion and man-made one ... and they claim the first explosion was definitely man made. Another fact is that both the naval base and the airbase had everything packed up ready to evacuate before the eruption."

"That's off the planet."

The scenery changed dramatically when we came over the mountains and down the freeway off ramp into Subic Bay. Sprawling out before us was the pretty little town. It rimmed the coastline of the impressive azure blue bay like lace lingerie.

The Yacht club was impressive with a splendid view of the marina and the Bay. Ricky drove into the underground car park. It felt good to be in a tropical resort away from the concrete jungle of Makati.

As it was lunchtime, we decided to eat at the Cambusa Bistro in the club and chose a window seat to try and guess which boat moored at the marina belonged to Raye and Nelson. After a satisfying feed of Western food, we checked into our respective rooms.

~~~

I was just settling back into a comfy armchair to read the newspaper when there was a knock at my door. Begrudgingly I got up and opened it.

"Sorry to disturb you boss but I got word on Gutierrez."

"Come in Ricky, sit down ... fill me in."

"Gutierrez has a share in a boat that's up for sale – it's also here."

"We're in luck then."

"It's cheaper to moor a boat here than at Manila Yacht Club," Ricky suggested.

"Go downstairs mate and check the guest register, see if any familiar names turn up over the last month. Also check marina security, I can't see any on the jetty from here. "

"Okay will do boss."

"I'll wait here."

I studied the topography of the marina from my window. Three wharves pointed out into Subic Bay like withered fingers. All of the moored boats were in full view of the yacht club and that presented a challenge for our intended unauthorized boarding.

After a while Ricky called from downstairs and suggested a drink by the pool. I didn't need my arm twisted and headed down.

~~~

As I stepped out the elevator I immediately spied a hot looking dish at reception. From behind, she looked good enough to eat. I lingered long enough to try and catch a gander of her front when suddenly she turned around. I ducked for cover when I recognized Bianca Gutierrez! Figuring Arnel might be close by, I quickly surveyed the lobby but saw no sign of him. Why would she be here alone, especially after yesterday's fiasco at Café Havana?

I slipped into the corridor that led to the pool.

Ricky had a Wallbanger waiting for me that badly needed a haircut. What is it with Yacht Clubs and vegetation?

"Guess who I just saw checking in?"

"Who boss?"

"Bianca Gutierrez."

"Well you won't believe this boss, all of them: Raye, Nelson and Arnel Gutierrez, have been here in the last four weeks, but only once."

"That makes a liar out of Nelson, he said he hasn't been here in months. I don't know about you Ricky but for me this case is getting crazier by the minute. Do we know who owns which boat?"

"Sure do boss."

"Any guards?"

"No security but sometimes a guard is posted on board by the owner."

"Phew, it's hot here," I complained.

We were exposed by the pool and needed to be less conspicuous with Bianca and possibly her brother lurking. We finished our drinks and agreed to have dinner in our rooms, and then to meet up at midnight in a dark alcove we'd identified just by the marina entrance. From there we'd deploy on a covert mission to search each of the boats.

Ricky left the elevator at his floor and I progressed to the upper deck. On the way to my room, a door opened in the corridor and Bianca stepped out. There was no avoiding her.

"Bee! Small world – fancy meeting you here," I said smoothly.

"I've nothing to say to you Stone!" She snapped.

"Mightn't have much to say but you've sure got plenty on show – a sight for sore eyes."

"Save the compliments Stone."

She went to walk away. With my cover blown, I needed to stop her from alerting Arnel. I stopped her with an outstretched arm, moved seductively closer and altered my tone to my best bedroom whisper.

"Look, I know we got off on the wrong foot ..."

"Excuse me, girls best friends are her legs bye."

She could get past me.

"But all good friend have to part sometime," I said with a warm smile. "Let me make it up to you. How about finishing that glass of champers – in my room?"

I sensed her resolve weaken.

"I don't feel dressed for cocktails."

"No need to change on my account, I like you just the way you are."

Her eyes flashed seductively.

We slipped into my room and she sat on the lounge while I fetched a half bottle of Veuve Clicquot from the minibar.

"Odd us both being here?" I popped the cork and filled two flutes.

"I know why I'm here, how about you?" She purred with a questioning raised eyebrow.

"I'm a member of the Royal Sydney Yacht Club," I lied. "They offered me a night here, and with it being the weekend ... " I handed her a flute – we touched glasses.

"Ah ha," she said doubtfully. "You're here alone?"

I had to lie again – I was making a habit of it with this dame.

"Yes. And you?" We sat at each end of the three-seat couch – worlds apart.

"Sometimes I come here on weekends when I need to escape Makati. We have a boat at the marina."

"Alone?"

"Sometimes I bring someone to play with ... but not this time."

"Hmm, I like to play."

Then before I realized it, she had put down her glass and slid along the couch until she was sitting right next to me. I could feel the vibrant flesh of her thigh pressing lightly against mine. Her lips were invitingly close, her fragrance exciting, and I asked myself, hell, why does a guy always think he has to work so hard creating the right atmosphere if the female passions were already beginning to stir from their slumbers?

"Well," she said sleepily. "What are you waiting for? Here I am, in your room, with soft lights and a mood that sends ripples up my spine and the drink brings out the primitive in me. Are you man or mouse or did you only want to ask me questions? Have I misjudged you?"

The invitation was too pressing to refuse – or even think about. I mean, what was I expected to do when she was making it so obvious? I put down my flute.

Our lips met, lightly at first, then with more force and feeling as our passions began to take over. They writhed and mashed against each other like living creatures. Her mouth opened and her cool, moist tongue pushed in between my lips, and then both our tongues were engaged in a fencing duel. Her hands were running up and down my waist, and her breasts were pressing firmly against my chest as she forced me back on the couch, as she rose on top of me, the hardness in my groin was complete. Our lips were glued together, and it was obvious that she was just as hungry as I was.

Her body was squirming on top of mine, and I rose to meet her. Her fingers were easing under my shirt and my skin tingled to the cool touch of her fingers. She was bringing my shirt away from the waistband of my pants. Her lips lightly touched my nipples, her tongue circled them, and her teeth gave me a gentle nip. Her fingers played skillful arpeggios all over my heated body, and I was quite happy to let her take the initiative. I slid my hands beneath her sweater and softly kneaded her firm breasts. She moaned and squirmed more passionately against me. I brought the sweater up over her breasts, and there they were above me, smallish and classically formed, the dark nipples swollen with her desire.

Straightening up from me, she rolled away and pulled off her sandals. Then she stood up, and unzipping her jeans, peeled them down over her thighs. She stepped out of them. My fully erect rod was throbbing with fierce intensity, and a sharp ache spread outward from my groin. She stood in front of me, her black sweater still hiked up over her breasts, and the only other thing she had on was a pair of flimsy black briefs that barely covered her pubis. With a cheeky half smile, and making a big production of it, she slowly drew the briefs down and kicked them away from her.

The sight was breathtaking. The dark jewel between her thighs seemed to sparkle in its invitation to me – her clit protruded from her moist slit like a baby's thumb and that was all I needed.

We rolled onto the couch, struggled and strained against each other, we dived and plummeted to fantastic depths. We were on a runaway train. We tasted each other and drank to the max. She gave little tremulous cries and her fingernails carved welts across my back, but I hardly noticed it. Her thighs gripped me in a tight embrace as I plunged deep into to her to the hilt, as she strove upward to meet me, to absorb me to the fullest extent. And I was driving deep, I don't know that she had been filled like this before: I was conquering a new world, smashing down barriers. I was Axis Stone rampant, triumphant, the greatest lover of all time. Her moans echoed in my ears.

Chapter Ten

I ordered dinner for two in the room – we needed sustenance after two hours of sublime fiery sex. After dinner, we couldn't resist each other and we made it again this time on the bed. Exhausted, we drifted off to sleep in an embrace.

I woke with a start and checked the time – it was 12.17 A.M., past the midnight rendezvous with Ricky! I dressed in a panic careful not to awaken sleeping beauty.

There was only one staff member at reception – other than that the lobby was void of life. I slipped past him without much effort and out through the big glass doors that opened onto the marina. Thirty or so boats were moored at the marina and only two had cabin lights on. That told me the rest were probably empty. I reached the dark alcove meeting point but Ricky wasn't there – then in the shadows I sighted a body face down on the ground. It had to be Ricky. I rolled him over and found the results of a terrible beating. Blood was dripping from the back of his head forming a pool on the ground that glistened in the light of the moon. I felt for a pulse and got it ... I was relieved – he was alive ... but only just – it was weak. I needed to call an ambulance quick smart and so took off on the double to get help from the lone receptionist.

~~~

I rode next to Ricky in the back of the ambulance to the Subic Medical Center, and then waited for what seemed like an eternity while an emergency team worked on him. Eventually a nurse emerged from ER and told me they'd stabilized him, and there was no point in me hanging round to come back later. I felt as guilty as hell. I'd let my friend down, the same guy that had saved my ass only nights before. The little head had ruled the big head and it wasn't the first time that had happened.

I decided to walk back to the Yacht Club to mull over things on the way, but the guilt followed me. Kicking stones I wondered who had attacked Ricky – maybe it was Arnel? Who knew our plans? Maybe he'd been mugged? I'd have to wait until Ricky came around to get the answers.

When I got to my room, I found the Bee had flown. Understandable, she'd probably awakened, found me gone and scurried back to her own room. The sun was up ... I was past being sleepy so I headed for a buffet breakfast at the Club café. On the way I knocked on Bianca's door. There was no answer I guessed she was sleeping.

As I got out of the elevator my phone vibrated ... it was Cortez.

"Hi Sancho, news travels fast. I didn't tell you I was coming here because ... Right, you're taking the chopper ... All right ... I'll see you there in three hours."

He was pissed off and rightfully so, I had taken things into my own hands again and this time someone got hurt. I would have to take it on the chin.

I was staring out the window of the café at the marina when my phone buzzed again, this time it was the hospital to say Ricky was out of danger and awake. It was good news.

~~~

By the time I entered the hospital room, Ricky already had guests: Cortez and two uniformed Subic Barangay cops. A nod from Cortez and the uniforms left the room. Ricky looked awful. His face was gray, battered and bruised with one eye swollen shut. His right hand was bandaged with his fingers in splints.

"Hey Ricky, glad to see you're alive and kicking. Has Cortez been giving you the third degree?"

It was difficult for him to talk but he tried his best.

"There were two of them boss," he groaned. "No faces ... balaclavas ... tire levers, one held my hand while the other one busted my fingers."

Wincing in pain he held up his injured right hand.

I winced – it looked painful. "Did they say anything?" I asked.

"Just my name, they called me and came from behind."

That meant they knew exactly who he was so it wasn't a mugging. A nurse entered and told us to leave. Cortez had one last question.

"Ricky, who else knew you were going to search the boats?"

The question obviously bothered Ricky; he didn't want to expose his contact at police HQ.

I chimed in. "Ricky, whoever you told almost certainly set you up."

"Where were you boss?"

"You'll have to leave now!" The nurse growled at us with insistence.

"I was with Bianca Gutierrez," I averted my eyes with guilt.

"Maybe she split us up on purpose," Ricky said through clenched teeth, the pain getting to him.

The reality of that idea struck me like a ton of bricks.

"My contact at HQ is Vic Cruz," Ricky admitted.

I recognized an immediate mood swing from Cortez at the mention of the name.

Cortez stormed out of the room.

"You get some rest Ricky."

I loped after Cortez.

"Sancho! Wait!"

He stopped outside the hospital and lit up a cigarette.

"What's up? It was the mention of Vic Cruz wasn't it?" I probed.

The cigarette calmed him down.

"There's a Starbucks a couple of blocks away, we'll talk there," he said irritably.

~~~

The uniforms gave us a lift to the Starbucks, and then waited outside for us. We grabbed a couple of coffees and sat down.

"So, tell me about Vic Cruz?"

"It is a story I thought you didn't need to know, but it is now relevant. My brother Pablo was an operative for the Philippine National Police Anti Illegal Drugs Group, which is headed up by Vic Cruz."

"He's the head of the nark squad?"

"Yes. Pablo was undercover in a drug ring suspected of being run by Ringo Raye. His cover name was Tony Lamont. There was a big Shabu deal going down, Pablo had been working on it for a year."

"Shabu?"

"Crystal meth. Pablo took a truck with a gang member to the high security enclosure of the Manila Container Terminal, and loaded a container harboring the drugs. He had informed his drug task force superior, and they planned to ambush the truck at the exit gate but the task force assembled at the wrong gate. Someone had informed on Pablo. As the truck was leaving the terminal, he was shot. The truck ran into the traffic, crashed and exploded. The mysterious passenger who shot him escaped before the explosion, Pablo was killed."

"I'm sorry for your loss ... Were the drugs destroyed?"

"The truck was gutted. I learned from forensics

that Pablo had been shot before the explosion. There was a bullet in his chest. He had been shot at point blank range."

"So where does Cruz fit in?" I asked.

"He was the commanding officer ... it was a co-operative effort between customs, the PDEA, Philippine Drug Enforcement Agency and the police ... since that time, I have tried to prove his complicity but to no avail."

"You mean you suspect he was in on it?"

"He must have been. It was Cruz that sent them to the wrong gate, and only he could have blown Pablo's cover."

"No police investigation?"

"Cruz is too powerful, way too connected with the underworld, senators ... you name it, anyone of influence and he's got something on them."

"How could he do that?"

"He's a law unto himself, answerable to no one. I give you an example. When Pablo was first recruited into the drug squad he worked directly under Cruz and after a while he took Pablo into his confidence and opened up to him – maybe he was bragging but anyhow ... he told Pablo that one time he needed a decision to go his way in court, so he found out who the judge would be on the day, planted drugs on his oldest son and then busted him. Of course the decision went his way. "

"So you're saying Pablo knew this about Cruz?"

"Yes, Pablo had enough evidence on Cruz to bury him. But Cruz's task force was formed directly by the president."

"Was Pablo planning on exposing him?"

"It's plausible."

"Were you working with Pablo to that end?"

"Let's just say we had a common interest."

"So there was no inquiry on the aborted drug bust?"

"Cruz swept it under the table. Look, if I was to accuse him of anything I would wind up in Manila Bay wearing concrete shoes."

"So you went after Raye?"

"Yes, I saved some of Pablo's files before Cruz could destroy them. They pointed the finger at Raye behind the deal without spelling his name out. But I figured if I could get Raye I could ultimately get Cruz."

"Raye must have lost a fortune in that fire?"

"They both did ... it was one of the biggest drug hauls ever in this country."

"Didn't Pablo tell anybody the name of his passenger?"

"Only Cruz would have known, which further implicates him ... he of course denies it. Later, my task force arrested Arnel Gutierrez on suspicion of conspiracy to murder from a tip off, but Cruz had him released within hours without charge or my knowledge."

"That's suspicious."

"There is more, the Vargas family owns and operates the high security container depot where the drugs arrived, and Bianca Gutierrez was Nick's girlfriend at the time."

"Jesus! This is all somehow connected to the kidnapping isn't it?" I said astounded.

We were at last getting somewhere, and Ringo was beginning to look decidedly ugly.

"I still want to search the boats," I told him anxiously.

"Who owns them?"

I pulled my phone. "Ricky texted me the info ... wait, right ... Ringo owns Bodyshot, Nelson has Go See and the Gutierrez family has Sarap. Can we get a search warrant?"

"No, can't help you there that is maritime services

jurisdiction. I am due back at HQ in an hour. I would be dropping that line of investigation if I were you Stone, seeing your intentions seem to be too well known."

"Yes, I think you might be right."

"They will release Ricky this afternoon. Best collect him and you two hightail it back to Makati quick smart."

"I hear yer."

~~~

The uniforms dropped me back at the Subic Yacht Club, and then took Cortez to the police helipad.

I went directly to Bianca's room. I needed to know if she'd set me up. After bashing on the door for five minutes I quit and went down to reception to ask if she'd checked out. I got an affirmative. Angry with myself I went to the swimming pool ordered a drink and sat on a deck chair staring mindlessly into space when I saw Sancho's police chopper flashing across the cerulean sky bound for Makati. That brought me back to reality and I focused my attention on the marina. I decided to take a stroll for a sly gander at the boats.

The blazing hot sun and the humidity had my armpits leaking like a faucet with a dud washer. There was little activity to be seen on the wharves. The first wharf obviously catered for the deluxe boats because of its proximity the amenities as a result the boats were bigger. The next wharf accommodated the middleclass moorings – smaller boats – and then the economy section. Thinking of Raye, I decided to check the deluxe wharf for his boat, Bodyshot. I tried to look as inconspicuous as my western frame would permit in the Philippines and strolled along the wharf with my hands clasped behind my back like Prince Philip, stopping and acting to peer into the green water for fish. I'd made it half way along when I sighted two unfriendly looking guards eyeballing me from the deck of a boat. I nonchalantly retreated and then continued along the middle class wharf and quickly came upon a Halvorsen Broadwater 32 with name Sarap on its stern. It was the boat the Gutierrez family used in syndicate with partners. I knelt down and messed with my shoelace while surreptitiously taking in the topography for a return visit later tonight. There didn't seem to be anyone aboard, so I carried on. At the end of the wharf, I found a Rhodes 27 sailing boat named Go See, again with no one on board. It was Nelson's style all right: a run-down old sucker its hull painted with barnacles.

~~~

I had only just entered my room when the phone rang. It was the hospital: Ricky was ready to be discharged.

Just on dusk, the uniforms dropped him at the Yacht Club, and I helped him up to my room. He could walk but only gingerly.

"We'll leave later tonight mate. I'll drive. But first, I'm going to search the boats like we planned," I told him firmly.

"Don't be crazy boss, it isn't safe on your own!"

"Let me worry about that mate. I've extended the checkout time, so just kick back and take it easy, I'll be back soon."

The sun had gone down and the lobby was deserted when I crossed it to slip out through the doors onto the marina. I made it undetected. But Ricky was right ... I could sense danger.

I walked quickly onto the wharf ... there was no one around just a boat tying up at the end of the closest one: the deluxe wharf.

When I climbed aboard Sarap, I found the cabin door open, so I crept inside. It took only minutes to determine there was nothing to be found. Next was Nelson's boat Go See. A yacht is much more difficult to board because it's far less sturdy than a cruiser. The damn thing rocked and rolled and I stumbled about in the dark like a blind man on a trampoline. I nearly ended up on my ass trying to step down from the deck onto the companionway. When I reached for the door handle to the cabin, it suddenly flew open and a big burly dude in a black balaclava dived out and tackled me around the legs. We hit the deck together with a thump. Built like a friggin" tank – he was getting the better of me until I managed to lift my knee into his groin. He immediately doubled up in pain groaning like he'd been castrated. I took the opportunity to split. As I jumped onto the gunwale he reached up from the deck, grabbed my trouser leg and lifted himself enough to land a massive kidney punch. I went down gasping for air. Standing over me, he let fly with a barrage of punches to my face. I felt a stream of warm blood running down my cheek ... the bastard had split my eyebrow. All I could think of was *how the stuff am I going get out of this?*

Chapter Eleven

The answer came from just above me and it wasn't heaven – it was the boom. I mustered all my strength ... deflected a vicious left hook from him with my forearm, struggled to my feet, grabbed the boom and swung it at him with all my strength. It caught him by surprise as he was getting to his feet and smacked him right across the bridge of the nose knocking him backwards base over apex. Proud of my work, I looked down at him sprawled out on the deck. He was out cold and urgently in need of rhinoplasty. Feeling pretty shabby after the beating he'd given me, I hoofed it as fast as my wobbly legs would carry me back to the sanctuary of the Yacht Club.

~~~

We were packed and on the Luzon Highway, driving south for Makati quicker than you could say Jack Robinson. There was no way I was going to hang around the Yacht Club to risk another beating – I liked my face the way it was before the Go See brawl. My mind was echoing with the thought why was I attacked on Go See. Did I need to promote Nelson to number one on my hit list of suspects? I was kicking myself for not getting the chance to check out Raye's boat, Bodyshot.

Ricky was asleep when we got to Balintawak: the off ramp from the freeway to Epifanio de los Santos or EDSA Avenue as it's known locally. I was only just managing to cope with driving on other side of the road when suddenly I found myself under siege from chaotic traffic. The lack of street signage and the confusion caused me to hit the panic button.

"Ricky! Wake up pal! There are friggin" roads

going everywhere, which one do I take for fuck's sake?"

He opened one badly bruised eye, yawned and then mumbled, "Turn right on EDSA, that's the big street boss, it will take us all the way to Makati." Then he promptly nodded off back to sleep.

~~~

I pulled the car into the Dela Rosa Apartments on Ayala Avenue, Makati and got the concierge to help Ricky up to his apartment. I thought it best to leave his car in the apartment car park and then walk to the Shang. By the time I reached it the humidity had my armpits leaking like a sieve.

Sporting a cut eyebrow and split lip, looking for all the world like I'd come from a prizefight I'd lost, I tried to slip through the reception area to the elevator without notice. As soon as I got into my room I dived into a steaming hot shower.

After cleaning up my wounds it was time to ring Lola Lovejoy for a progress report. Her warm, sultry voice answered and the hairs on my forearms stiffened with excitement.

"Lola, hi ... it's Axis."

"I've been worried about you, it's been ..."

"I'm fine," I cut her off. "Ricky my off-sider and I took a bit of a beating but we're all right. Have you heard anything?"

"I can't believe what you just said! You took a beating? My lord! Why?"

"Oh, an occupational hazard ..." I played it up big to get some sympathy.

"Are you hurt?"

"Just a split lip and a few bruises, Ricky spent the night in the hospital and has a few broken fingers but he'll live. So, have you heard anything from the kidnapper?"

"No, we haven't heard a thing ... we're running out

of time aren't we?"

"We are ... but I reckon he'll take us right down to the wire and call you tomorrow."

"Do you have any news to tell Dad? Anything, please I don't want to just tell him you guys took a beating, it will only make him worry more."

"Tell him I've established a good working relationship with the cop in charge, Sancho Cortez, and that we've narrowed it down to three suspects, but we need conclusive evidence before we can make a move on any of them."

"Oh Axis," she whimpered. "I don't know what I'd do without you."

I wished she knew what to do with me, because I sure as hell know what I'd do with her.

"Just tell your Dad things are progressing. Call me as soon as you hear something, okay?"

"Thank you Axis, good night." She threw me a kiss through the phone and it landed like a left hook. If there's one thing talking to a sexy broad on the phone does it's fire me up. The idea that Bianca had set me up was still nagging at me. I checked the phone numbers Ricky had given me, found hers and rang. When it answered it was Bianca but she quickly handed the phone over to someone else.

"Who's this?" A male voice asked.

"Axis Stone, is that you Arnel?"

"You've got the wrong number."

I knew it was Arnel.

"Hey don't go way! I know it was you that hit Ricky at the Yacht club. Do you know how I know? Because it was a fuckin' cowardly attack ... and you're a fucking coward ... So let me tell you what I'm going to do about it ... I'm coming after you shit for brains ... And know this ... I've got the skill set to fuckin' kill you ... Now you might argue you have the same ... Well then, one way or another we're going to find out aren't we?"

"Go fuck yourself Stone!" He growled and hung up.

At least I'd got it off my chest and issued a challenge. It felt good ... now to deal with the next quandary. Why had I been attacked on Go See? The finger was firmly pointed at Nelson. I know he's doing it tough, but is that motive enough for him to kidnap Kitty? I checked his number and rang him.

A babe answered.

"Hello."

"Hi, I want to speak with Buddy Nelson? Tell him it's Axis Stone private investigator."

She went to get him and I could hear him in the background berating her for not giving me the flick.

"What do you want Stone?" He growled.

"We need to talk," I snarled back.

"I've got nothing more to say to you."

"Unless you want to get busted for aiding and abetting a kidnapping, I suggest we talk ... and real soon."

There was a pregnant pause while he considered his options – he didn't have any.

"All right Stone, have it your way, hop a cab to my apartment. I'll text you the address."

This time I packed my piece unwilling to take any chances with this asshole.

~~~

The cabbie found Colonnade Residences on Legazpi Street, and I went inside. It was an old style, Spanish looking block with a rickety old elevator servicing the nine floors. A fake Roman plaque finished in gold leaf gilt identified the door to Nelson's suite, number 66. I knocked loudly then waited. After what seemed like ages, the door opened just enough for me to see a pair of ice blue eyes staring coldly at me.

"What the hell do you want?" The voice belonging

to the eyes asked. I pushed the door open wider – her red hair was long and spread in wild profusion around her shoulders. She was wearing a thin crimson silk robe, belted around her waist ... the hem reached the middle of her thighs. Her breasts were full, and the thin silk outlined her large nipples. She was exotic looking, maybe Russian with serious bedroom eyes.

"The name's Stone, I'm here to meet Buddy Nelson."

"He's not here," she snapped arrogantly with a heavy eastern block accent. She tried to close the door in my face but I jammed it with my foot.

"Hey, I haven't finished talking. When will he be back?" I growled.

"I have no idea." The arctic tone of her voice didn't go at all with the Manila humidity. I saw no point trying to talk logic with her, that would be about as stupid as trying to catch a cab on a rainy day.

"Is there a problem Zelda?" A male voice resounded from some place in back of her.

"A dude called Stone," she grunted. "Wants to talk with Buddy, he says."

"I'll take care of it."

"I'd be glad if you did," she called out frigidly. "The way he's staring at me now I figure wearing a robe is a complete waste of time."

She turned away and I watched the tight bounce of her high-riding butt under the thin tight silk for a couple of exhilarating seconds before she disappeared.

Her place was taken by the owner of the male voice: a young Filipino hunk in his mid-twenties with unruly black hair and built like a Sherman tank ... obviously a bodybuilder.

"I'm Al Perez," he said. "You are?"

"Stone, Private investigator, are you hard of hearing?"

"So?" He raised his upper lip with a snarl.

"I spoke with Buddy, he invited me here."

"Fascinating!" He yawned carefully. "Your client wouldn't be Nick Vargas would it?"

"My client's identity is confidential. Can I come in?"

"No way," he said curtly. "Got any ID?"

I sighed annoyed, pulled my wallet and flashed my license. He wasn't impressed.

"Goodbye Stone," he growled.

My foot was still in the doorjamb so he couldn't slam it shut.

"Out!" He yelled and grabbed my shoulder. "You just ran out of time, Stone!"

I was wearing boots so I kicked him hard in the shin. He let out a yelp and hopped about on one foot with both hands clasping his shin. I chopped the edge of my hand down across the side of his neck real hard. He went down onto the floor flat-out and stayed there.

The Rusky came running right at me like a screaming banshee, her hands hooked into claws, her long nails driving toward my face. A tall strong looking girl around five ten it was ugly. Now as a rule I don't hit women but this was going to be an exception. I smacked her on the chin just hard enough to stop her in her tracks.

A voice rang out from behind me.

"What are you doing to my actors Stone?"

I turned to find him behind me, "Just giving them some direction Nelson, they'd crossed the line."

He pushed his big frame past me, stepped over the big hunk on the deck and put a consoling arm around the Rusky.

"Zer bastard hit me," she whimpered angrily.

"Self defense," I countered.

"I can believe that ... she can be a tigress our Zelda, it's that Baltic blood," he mumbled peering down at

Perez sitting on the floor scratching his head confused like someone had stolen his ice cream and he didn't know why. "Give him a hand into the bedroom Zelda, I need to talk with Stone."

She put her hands on hips and protested, "Why the fuck should I ..."

"Watch your mouth Zelda, because I goddamned told you so – that's why," he reprimanded loudly. "No arguments."

Pulling a scowling dark face, she helped Perez to his feet and off into the bedroom.

Nelson sat down in his favorite armchair and motioned for me to sit in a two-seater opposite him. Impeccably dressed, around fifty and overweight, he stared at me with insolent distain.

"What's this about Stone?" He asked in the kind of voice that strongly doubted it was possible.

"I was at the Subic Bay Yacht Club earlier today and paid your boat Go See a visit and got this as a reward," I protested pointing at my cut eyebrow.

"That's what you get for sticking your fucking eyebrow into someone else's business." His voice gained added confidence from the slight wheedling tone I'd injected into my own, and a condescending smile spread his lips. "Go See! Ha! The last time I was in Subic I didn't even see her myself."

"You were there only weeks ago, are you asking me to believe you have nothing to do with the boat?"

"You're damn right I am ... you never stop spending fuckin' money on an old clinker like that piece of shit – want to buy it?"

"That's probably the worst sales pitch I've ever heard."

"You were looking for Kitty on my boat weren't you? You could've just asked me if she was on it. Why would I want to goddamn kidnap her?"

"Money."

"Ha! What fuckin' money?" He snapped.

"The kidnapper wants two million US."

"Hope he isn't holding his breath to get it."

"Now why would you say that?"

He leaned back crossed his big legs and checked the fingernails on his pudgy hands like he didn't give a rats ass. "Oh, a while ago I needed an investor for a big concert here and asked Kitty if her family would buy in. She laughed, and she said after her mother had died a few years back and her father ..."

"Winston."

"Yeah Winston, started playing the Gee Gees and got his fingers badly burnt."

The news rocked me back in my chair. It could explain Winston's ill health.

"So he lost a few bucks at the races. So what?"

"A few bucks? Ha! Word is it he owes millions to the Gold Coast bookies. He's so desperate it's common knowledge he can be bought to fix trials."

"You're having me on!"

"Not likely ... put it this way Stone," he eyeballed me with a sarcastic grin on his ugly fat mush. "You better have got your fee up front." He laughed and his jowls bounded up and down like jelly. His quivering jowls giving the impression of an overweight bloodhound, and come to think of it, that's something you don't see very often.

"Are you saying he wouldn't be able to pay the ransom?" I snapped.

"You got that part right pal," he chuckled finding it all most amusing.

That set me back in my chair ... it was the last thing I wanted to hear.

Nelson was far too slimy to be trusted. But he was now off my list of suspects. Kidnapping wasn't his speed, but after what he'd told me, I now had serious doubts about Winston's solvency. I needed to make sure I wasn't going to be the loser out of this gig.

Chapter Twelve

I had just left Nelson's apartment block and was heading back towards the Shang, when my phone rang and I answered.

"Stone. Yeah, Ringo, I'm in Makati. Where are you? Twin Towers on Ayala Avenue, yeah, I know where that is ... what's this about? Okay, catch you there in fifteen minutes."

That's how long it would take for me to walk from Legazpi Street to Twin towers at midnight.

As I strolled the sidewalk, I wondered what Ringo was up to. Was he just using me to keep in touch with the investigation? Was he setting me up? A cunning fox with motive, he definitely had the means to put a kidnapping together. Everything that happened at Subic Bay could've been part of an elaborate plan by him to put me off the scent. Is he in partnership with Cruz? Why was Bianca there? Why did she checkout of the yacht club without saying a word? Were Ringo and the Gutierrez family in league with the kidnapping? I was convinced a little more time spent socializing with Ringo at great risk to my person, could either produce answers to some of these nagging questions or have me pushing up daisies.

~~~

I entered Ringo's ritzy penthouse apartment. He wasn't alone. There were three babes lazing about on lounges in various stages of undress posing like Penthouse centerfolds.

"Having a party?" I questioned checking out the skin on show.

"Nothing out of the ordinary," he said with an arrogant smirk. He made his way to a well-stocked cellaret. "How about a bodyshot, Stone, ever had one?"

"Nope, but it sounds a smidgen dangerous."

"Oh, it is ... but well worth the risk, I promise you."

He waved for one of the girls to move to a vacant three-seat sofa.

"Our guest will have a bodyshot Suzy."

Moving like a panther she sat on the sofa, then reclined in a pose ever so vulnerable. Ringo approached her carrying a bottle of Russian Vodka.

"Come Axis, experience one of our Manila delights."

I joined him beside the supine girl. He filled a jigger with vodka, pulled her dress up to just under her breasts and then topped up her navel cavity with vodka.

"There, a bodyshot ... drink my friend."

I got the idea, leaned down and lapped up the warm liquid. It tasted excellent.

By the time I slurped a bodyshot from the navel orifice of each of the three girls, twice, I was feeling pretty loaded. It was a heady experience.

"So, which girl tasted the best Stone?"

"Suzy," I said without giving it much thought.

"Suzy, go to the guest room. Rita, Julie, go to my room."

I watched the three girls waddle off obediently – and thought – now the reason for the invite.

"I heard your ex-cop friend met with an accident."

"You mean Ricky? Yeah, he got mugged."

"You were in Subic?"

"Let's stop beating around the bush Ringo, you know where I was – what I want to know is ... what's your game?"

"I don't play games Stone, I invent them."

"We just played bodyshot, so I guess that either makes you a liar or a hypocrite."

"I didn't invent the bodyshot Stone ... Anyhow, they're tough words for someone who knows my reputation," he growled rotating one of the many rings decorating his fingers, obviously irritated. "I made it clear to you, my only interest is in finding Kitty."

"What about your interest in Tony Lamont? And what about your connection with the Gutierrez family?"

He sat back in the lounge chair peering at me through squinted eyes.

"Questions like that could get you killed."

"An occupational hazard."

"All right, I'll play along with your little game Stone. I don't have anything to do with the Gutierrez family, if you did your homework, you'd know they were partners at one time with Vargas. And as for Tony Lamont ... never heard of him. Your serve."

"What about Bianca?"

"Before she fastened her gold digging claws into Vargas, I had a roll between the sheets with her a few times. But for me, she's high maintenance."

"A few times – from what I've heard you were a regular donor."

"As you can see Stone," he motioned with his hand towards the bedroom. "I make regular donations to many receivers."

"Are you partners with Vic Cruz?"

"I have a lot of partners Stone."

"But this one's a cop, head of the Philippines National Police Anti-Illegal Drugs Group. Does that ring a bell Ringo?"

"Now do I look like the sort of guy that would have anything to do with narks or any government agency? You're barking up the wrong tree Stone."

"You've already demonstrated your influence with the cops getting me out of the clink."

"Bribing the cops is a way of life here ..."

I wasn't getting anywhere ... he was far too clever to trip up with that line of questioning, besides I felt he was becoming impatient.

"I need to check your boat," I said forcibly.

"For Kitty, ha! Be my guest, I'd be thrilled and surprised if you find her on it."

We sized each other up. Ringo had calmed down. I knew his type – even in a fistfight he'd remain calm. Guys like him were seriously scary, no guilt, no fear with no scruples.

He reached into his jacket – I flinched thinking he was going for a gun but was relieved when he pulled out a Havana cigar and lit it up. Puffing away to get it going, he blew a symbolic ring of smoke in the air and then fixed his shark-like eyes on me.

"Did Nelson kidnap her?"

"Unlikely, he hasn't got the balls or readies for the entrance fee. Why would Vargas kidnap her? She's already his girl ... and he doesn't need the ransom."

He held his chin in deep thought and puffed the cigar.

"It must be Cortez. There is no one else."

"So you think Cortez has the knowledge to set up a complicated transfer."

"Sure, they investigate cop corruption here all the time."

I decided to probe a little deeper.

"Do you know anything about Winston Lovejoy's gambling debts?"

"I've heard rumors."

"Would that put him in the mix?"

"I wouldn't discount it. That's enough, time for some fun. You take the guest room." He stood and put out his cigar in the ashtray. It symbolically marked the end of the discussion and he disappeared into his bedroom.

I wandered into the guest room and found Suzy sitting on the edge of the bed garbed in a white cheongsam split right up to her hip and with a shot glass of vodka in her hand. I sat down beside her. She tilted her glass to her lips and I saw the apple in her throat jump convulsively.

Without muttering a word she pushed the empty glass into my hand.

I took it to the en-suite bathroom without being stupid enough to ask her if she'd like a refill. When I got back to the living room she was standing beside the bed, prodding it carefully. Her hands disappeared behind her back and I heard the snick as the zipper parted. The next moment the silk dress was a soft heap around her ankles. She stepped out of it and kicked off her shoes leaving her in a lacy white bra and a matching string. Then she unhooked her bra and shrugged her shoulders so it fell to the floor. Freed of restraint, her full breasts jutted comfortably with the small brown nipples hard and elongated. Then she walked towards me until her full breasts came to an abrupt stop against my chest. I put my arms around her, holding her closer so her breasts squashed yieldingly against me. Her parted lips met mine, her tongue making a fierce darting exploration. I slid my hand down across the small of her back, under the tight elastic waistband of her string panty until the full globes of her bottom were tightly clasped with my fingers digging into the warm resilient flesh.

She made a hard sound deep inside her throat and then her questioning fingers undid my zip and dived inside. My rigid cock, freed from imprisonment reared in her tightly clutching hands. Standing on her tiptoes she pulled her lips away from mine.

I got the message and got out of my clothes in something like five seconds flat. By that time, Suzy was out of her string. The clean-shaven brown slit exposed held an attraction all of its own. She came straight back into my arms so my cock was pressed hard against the soft curve of her belly and her arms were wound around my neck. Her lips made a seal against mine and the weight of her breasts was a kind of fluid warmth against my chest. I cupped the cheeks of her bottom again firmly with both hands and, after a while, when my cock just couldn't stand the suspense any longer, I lifted her. Our mouths parted and she gave a grunt of approval as her elbows found leverage across my shoulders. When I lifted high enough, she wound both legs around my waist and then, as my questing rod homed in, I felt the moist warmth of her parting vaginal lips. She made a sharp woofing sound as she exhaled the moment the full length was inside her. It filled her to capacity. Still clamped inside her, I carefully lowered both of us on the bed. From a slow rhythmic beginning we built up to a thunderous climax with the bedsprings changing a chorus.

"I'm coming!" Suzy screamed, and had she waited a couple of seconds longer she could have spoken for both of us. For the next few seconds we were both transfixed on our mutual orgasm and then she slowly relaxed. Her whole body went limp and she fell forward on top of me. Her statement *I'm coming* was all she said to me, and I can't remember saying anything to her. I slid out from under her, went and took a shower in the en-suite. After I dressed, I noticed she'd fallen asleep and so left the apartment.

~~~

I rode the elevator down the twenty-five floors to ground and walked out into daylight. As I strolled in the dawning of the day, I figured I was none the wiser after talking to Ringo; if anything, I was more confused. The thought of old man Lovejoy being a suspect was seriously doing my head in.

I decided to have breakfast at Pancake House in

Greenbelt, as it was the only joint open at that hour. I knew I was in for a long day. Time would be up on the ransom demand soon, and I was no closer to finding Kitty. Ringo was pointing the finger at Cortez; Nelson at Winston Lovejoy; Cortez at Cruz; and me at the Gutierrez family. All the while poor old Ricky was at home licking his wounds. Sweat beaded up on my brow at the panicked thought I'd made a serious mistake calling the kidnapper's bluff. I headed back to my hotel room to sit it out.

I drifted off to sleep and was blown out of bed at eleven A.M., by the dulcet ringtone of The Terrible Tango. It was Lola, and she was in a terrible panic.

"Axis ... oh my God what are we going to do?" She bleated.

"Lola ... you've obviously heard from him, settle down. What did he say?" I mumbled sleepily.

"We heard all right, and it wasn't very pleasant."

I don't know what she was expecting but it certainly was never going to be pleasant.

"So tell me?" I urged and then yawned, blinking my eyes trying get my faculties together. I'm a slow starter.

"That he would only deal with one person, so we nominated you and gave him your cell number."

"Go on."

"He will text you the general location for the exchange. Once you text him that you're there in position, he'll text you after that with the exact location. Kitty will be there in full view but ..." She whimpered. "Oh Axis, he said she will be wired to an explosive device that can be triggered remotely if anything goes wrong!"

It wasn't sounding good – no wonder she was in a panic.

"Go on," I said calmly. "Take it easy."

There was a pause while she collected herself. "He

said he would then give us fifteen minutes to transfer the money, only when it's received will he disarm the bomb," she started to cry. "What are we going to do Axis? We don't have that kind of money."

"Sorry to be a realist kid, but you really only have one choice now."

"You're not listening me Axis, we don't have the money."

"I'm hearing you fine, but not having the money doesn't change anything. Look, why not contact Nick Vargas and ask him to loan you the bread. He's in love with Kitty and has the readies. I'll text you his number but you'll have to move fast."

"But I don't know if Dad will agree to any more debt, he's already ..."

"The clock is ticking Lola. Talk to Winston – make a decision and phone me back. I'll wait for your call ... and listen, while you're at it how about making sure my fee is covered."

"Okay will do, thank you Axis, bye."

When I terminated the call it was with the realization that Nelson had been spot-on: the Lovejoy's were up to their ears in financial woes. They were now faced with a massive decision: call the kidnapper's bluff or go deeper in debt. In my book there wasn't much choice really.

Chapter Thirteen

After I texted Lola the number for Nick Vargas, I phoned Cortez.

"Sancho, it's Axis Stone. We've had contact.

"Thank goodness."

"Yeah, it was looking grim for a while there. Anyhow, they've made me the point person and I'll be getting exchange instructions by text.

"When?"

"I don't know, when he's ready I guess."

"How do you want to play it?"

"Well, it doesn't sound like we'll have a lot of choice. He'll have Kitty wired to a bomb that can be remotely detonated. Once the money is in his account he'll deactivate it."

"Do you believe that?"

"Not at all, but we don't much choice do we?"

"I suppose you're right. Any more ideas on his identity?" He asked.

"Nothing. How about you? Any word on Cruz?" I queried.

"He's been out of town the last two weeks."

"That sounds suspiciously timely. But it doesn't fit in with Ricky talking to him."

"Unless Ricky calls his cell-phone," Cortez suggested.

"Yeah, that makes sense. He could be our man. Look, if he is, then he can't be working alone. Chicki Dee said two guys bundled Kitty into a waiting car, that's three counting the driver."

"And two guys attacked Ricky in Subic," Cortez added.

"Exactly."

This guy Cruz was rattling the Richter scale at nine.

"Better grill some of his colleagues," I pushed.

"That's easier said than done amigo."

"Hate to say it Sancho, but that's your job."

"Okay, okay, I'll do it. But what about the ransom ... have the Lovejoy's got it? Word is they are not traveling well financially."

"Seems everyone knew about that except me. I've put Lola Lovejoy in touch with Vargas maybe he'll kick the bin."

"It is a lot of loot for even someone like him. He won't be able to arrange that much quickly."

"I'm sure a millionaire like him has ways, anyhow we can't do much about it, I didn't think your department or the government would pay it."

"Ha, now you're being a comedian. Call me as soon as you hear something, okay?

I rang to check on Ricky. He was okay, just frustrated at being stuck at home.

"Did you ever get help from anyone else at Cruz's office?" I badgered him.

"No, only Cruz boss."

"Did you call him on a cell phone?"

"Yes, and I've tried the number a few times but it has been disconnected."

"Right ... did you have to pay him for information?"

"Sometimes, but mostly it was an exchange of favors, you know the drill boss."

"Do you know him personally Ricky?"

"Of course, he was my boss when I was in the force."

"Were you a nark?" I said surprised.

"Ten years in road patrol, three in the special drug squad."

"Why did you leave?"

"A bust went bad and a cop got killed. I got blamed for messing up."

"Was that cop Pablo Cortez?"

"Yeah, how did you know?"

I played on a hunch, "Ricky, listen to me this is important ... were you in charge of the task force for that bust?"

"Yes, I sure was."

"So you took the rap for being in the wrong place to ambush the truck?"

"Yes, and that got Pablo killed," he said sorrowfully.

"Who told you what gate to be at?"

"My superior operating officer, Vic Cruz."

My phone beeped.

"Hang on Ricky, I've got another call."

"Hello. Hi Lola, just a sec, I've got Ricky on hold." I switched back, "Ricky, I've gotta go it's the Lovejoy's, call you back later ... but it looks to me like your buddy Cruz is our kidnapper." I switched back, "Lola, sorry ... what's up?"

"Dad agreed to take on the debt, so I called Nick Vargas. He's a nice man ... he said not to worry and for you to call him to make the arrangements."

"Cool. I'll get onto him."

"Oh, by the way, the kidnapper said he will use MK as his ID when he texts you," she said.

"Okay, sit tight kiddo this is the tough part. I'll be in touch."

"Axis."

"Yes."

"Your fee is safe."

"I'm pleased to hear that but it would be even safer in my bank account with the deposit."

"I'll see what I can do. Please be careful."

"I'll do my best Lola ... bye."

I rang Vargas.

"Nick? It's Axis Stone."

"You must have spoken with Lola?" He said.

"Yes, so how do you want to play it?" I asked.

"I need to put a few things in place at the bank and that will take an hour or so. Call me as soon as you get the location."

"Done."

I decided to pack my bag confident the location for the exchange wouldn't be in Makati. Just then The Terrible Tango signaled an incoming text. I knew it was the kidnapper – it read: *Batangas MK*. I had no idea where that was so I Googled it. Even though it was only a hundred clicks from Makati that would make it at least a two-hour drive. I'd have to hire a car. I rang Nick back.

"Nick, I've just heard from him, it's a place called Batangas."

"Where in Batangas?" He probed.

"He didn't say ... just Batangas."

"What happens next then?" He prompted.

He sounded half-hearted but I pressed on regardless.

"Under normal circumstances, I'd have the cops triangulate his cell-phone seeing I have his number but I don't think that would be a good idea."

"I agree."

"So I need to get there, text him and he'll text me back the final location obviously somewhere in the area – is this Batangus a big place?"

"Yes ... and it's a tough call asking you to drive there and then find the location. Maps are not accurate and you're a foreigner. I'll take you."

"No, he only wants to deal with me."

"It's my money Axis, I insist."

"Can't argue with that. Okay, where, when and how?"

"I will meet you at the helipad on the Peninsula Hotel roof in three hours, we'll fly to Batangas ... I'll have a car meet us there."

"Now you're talking."

Nick had raised the bar. I had time to burn so I called Ricky back.

"Ricky."

"Boss. I've been thinking about what you said and I think you're right ... Cruz could be our man."

"Yeah, so what convinced you of that?"

"Something that always bothered me ... Cruz is a rich man, not from old money like Vargas but money he earned as a cop, and as you know we get paid a mere pittance, so how did he get it? I always believed he was on the take, and I think he was in on that drug bust."

"That would make him partners with Ringo, if Cortez is right and Ringo the mastermind."

"Another thing worries me ... Bianca Gutierrez was the fiancé of Vargas at the time and the Vargas family owns and operates ATI, Asian Terminals Inc., where the container holding the drugs was stored."

"Yeah, that's understandable."

"Well, someone had to give the truck access in and out of the terminal."

"You think that was Bianca?" I questioned.

"It sure makes sense."

"It makes as much sense as someone like Cruz blowing the whistle on Pablo to whoever was in the truck with him to have him whacked. Two birds with the one stone."

"I'm pretty sure I know who that was."

"Who?"

"Arnel Gutierrez."

Ricky was on the money. It could only be Arnel. That's probably the only reason Bianca had done the dirty on Vargas, to arrange free passage for the truck in and out of the high security container terminal.

"Maybe Kitty learned the secret and that's why

Ringo, Cruz and the Gutierrez's need to get rid of her."

"And maybe they want their money back from the drugs that went up in smoke first."

"That's it Ricky even the figures match, two mill worth of drugs, two mill ransom, now all we need do is prove it. I'm leaving in a couple of hours to make the exchange."

"Where is it?"

"I can't say, Ricky."

"I understand boss. Just remember they would want Kitty dead. I don't think they have any intention of returning her alive."

"Good advice Ricky, something I'll have to take into account. I'll call you when and if I survive this shit."

"I hear you boss. Be careful."

"And listen, if it does go tits up and you don't hear from me by noon tomorrow, call Cortez and tell him everything we've just talked about."

"You can count on me boss. By the way you said hitting Pablo was killing two birds with the one stone, what did you mean by that?"

"There was more than one reason why Cruz and Raye would want Pablo dead. One was he was going to blow the whistle on Cruz."

"You know that idea adds a very troublesome possibility to this case boss."

"Yeah, what's that?"

"Cruz would have connections all the way to the president, his task forced was appointed by him."

"Yeah, so?"

"With that sort of influence you will need to watch your tail, if things don't go Cruz's way he could call up a favor from pretty high up, if you get my drift."

"Yeah, I'm with you Ricky."

I hung up thinking I've never been in a spot like this before and it certainly wasn't looking good.

The house phone rang and the front desk clerk said they had a Miss Gutierrez in the lobby. I asked for her to be sent up.

A knock at the door, I opened it to find her dressed in a black silk shirt and a white linen skirt: a cute outfit.

"Well," I said. "You finally turn up. Enter."

She came in. I checked the corridor to make sure she was alone – then closed the door.

"I have some questions for you and no buts!" I said sternly.

She looked at me doubtfully, and then caught the full impact of my facial expression.

"Try me," she said throwing herself down on the couch.

"All I want from you is the truth," I snarled.

She sat back in the sofa with her arms folded defiantly.

"Fire away," she grunted.

"Did you arrange permission for the truck to enter and then leave the Asia Container Terminal?"

"Maybe I did, maybe I didn't. What's it to you?"

"Who was in that truck?" I pressed.

"They said on the news it was an undercover cop. He got killed."

"Who was with him in the truck?" I pushed.

"I don't know," she snapped.

"Who was behind the whole thing?"

"I have no idea. Look, what's this all about? I came here to tell you something, not to get the once over from you."

I realized I should take it easy on her. But I was running out of time, Vargas was due in about thirty minutes. I pulled up an armchair opposite her and sat.

"One last question, did you use me as a diversion at Subic Bay so someone could beat up my partner?"

"You said you came alone?"

"Just answer the question."

"No."

"Okay, I'm all ears. Spit it out."

"Look, I've probably played my cards wrong up till now, I've had my chances and blown them big time."

"You mean with Vargas."

"Yes, and other situations ... Sometimes you start with all the right intentions but forces pull you this way and that ... and then you end up doing everything wrong, it all fucks up and there's no going back."

"You talking about Ringo or Arnel?"

"Whoever, family ... people – they can all have an emotional grip on you."

"Okay, go on, I'm listening," I assured her.

"People have been hurt, killed even and now there's a kidnapping, I feel responsible for starting it all ..."

"The entry and exit permit for the truck?"

She started to cry.

"I just don't want anyone else to get hurt, that's all."

I wasn't sure whether to console her or not ... maybe that's what she wanted: a shoulder to cry on.

"What are you saying?" I probed.

"I don't want you and Kitty killed."

I stood up.

"Do you know something I don't?" I pressed her.

"Kitty knows too much, just like me. So that makes us targets."

I was getting the picture and it wasn't pretty but it was time to leave.

"Why now? Why are you telling me this?"

She put her face in her hands and wept.

I stood. "Look, I've got to go ... I've got an important meeting in ten minutes."

She looked up – her eyes red – nose running.

"Please don't go Axis," she pleaded.

"I gave you a chance, you admitted nothing, now I'm out of here."

I opened the door for her. She got up and slowly walked towards me. When she reached me, she stood on her tiptoes and gently pecked me on the lips.

"I told you because I'm pregnant. When I told Nick, he asked if I wanted to keep it, I said no. He knows I have no money." She started crying again. "He's such a good guy ... he sent me five thousand dollars to go to Hong Kong for an abortion. I don't want him to know that I'd taken advantage of him, that's all."

"Guilt is a terrible thing Bianca, but you're going to have to live with that."

I couldn't be bothered asking the name of the father.

"Can you talk to him for me Axis?" She pleaded.

"It's time you grew up and sorted out your own life Bee."

I closed the door at back of me, walked her to the elevator and pressed the call button.

"Good luck kiddo," I said patting her on the ass into the elevator.

She turned inside and with teary eyes said, "Nothing is what it seems Axis, don't get yourself killed."

The elevator door closed leaving me pondering the conundrum: *nothing is what it seems?*

Chapter Fourteen

With my port in my hand I called the next elevator, rode it down to ground then slipped out of the West Street exit of the Shangri-La. The traffic was heavy which made it relatively easy to slip between cars across Ayala Avenue to The Peninsula Hotel.

The Peninsula grand lobby made me think I'd been staying in the wrong hotel, but I didn't have time to linger and went directly to reception. They jumped to attention at the mention of Vargas and a boy in a white suit, with matching gloves and a pillbox hat appeared to lead me to the rooftop helipad.

We stepped out onto the tarmac just as the Bell 429 touched down. I raced over, ducked under the rotating blades and climbed on board the seven-seat chopper.

Nick greeted me with a helmet fitted with coms, so we could have a three-way conversation with the pilot. We lifted off.

"My pilot Dan Ilagan, is ex-military and will provide tactical support for the hand-over."

"Excellent. But we'll need to be careful. The kidnapper is only expecting me."

"No problem," Dan replied.

"I had a visit from Bianca," I said.

"I heard from her yesterday," Nick added with a single raised eyebrow.

"Yes, I know all about it. But she didn't drop by to tell me just that, she came to warn me."

"Warn you? What about? She wouldn't know about this ... unless."

"No, I've told nobody. She left me with a conundrum: *Nothing is what it seems ...*"

"What do you supposed that means?" Nick asked.

"She is a bit of a scatter-brain you know?"

"Yeah, but I think she was trying to tell me the kidnapper plans to kill Kitty and me."

"How would she know that?"

"I got her to admit that she arranged access for the truck driven by Pablo Cortez into your security container terminal to pick up the drugs."

"What?" He was shocked.

"Yes, I believe she did it for her brother, who I suspect was working for Ringo at the time. I also believe Raye was and maybe still is in league with Vic Cruz, head of the special drug force. I think Cruz blew the whistle on Pablo ... the undercover agent driving the truck, who incidentally was the brother of Sancho Cortez ... and sent the drug squad to the wrong gate for the ambush which resulted in his death and two million in drugs going up in flames with the truck."

"My God, do you realize what you're saying?" Vargas shouted to get above the engine noise.

"I sure do. That puts Cruz behind the kidnapping and possibly Raye. I think Kitty knows too much about it ... and that why he intends to kill her as soon as the ransom is in the bank."

"This is madness. That means he's definitely planning on killing you as well."

"Sure does ... I think it's how the consortium means to get the two mill back they lost when the dope went up in smoke."

I glanced out of the window at the beautiful countryside below. We were flying over a volcanic crater filled with the bluest water.

"What's that?"

"Taal, beautiful isn't it?"

"Yeah, hope I get to see it on the way back."

Nick got the inference.

We landed on a resort helipad in Anilao, Batangas.

Once the rotors had stopped we deplaned.

We strolled in the warm afternoon sun towards a well-camouflaged dark wood-paneled building nestled in the tropical vegetation.

"This is Eagle Point Resort, it's owned by a friend of mine," Nick said. "I figured it would make a good HQ. I have a Pajero here, and Dan has arranged three more armed men. Did you tell Cortez the plan?"

"No. I thought it best not to have any police interference."

"I'm glad you made that decision. You're getting savvy to ways of us Filipinos my friend."

"I think survival instinct has caused that," I agreed.

~~~

Inside the Nordic style hotel lobby, that made me check around for a Swedish masseuse, we instead found the resort manager, Frank Concepcion, a cultured mestizo Filipino in his mid-fifties with a well-schooled British accent and affable manners. He sent us to a six-bedroom bungalow reserved for Nick. I got the distinct impression that Eagle Point was one of Nick's regular haunts: maybe for the odd dirty weekend. The three troopers and Dan were billeted next door in a smaller bungalow.

An hour later we met up to discuss a strategy. The day felt longer than a state burial, and as the waters of Balayan Bay began to glow with the dying orange embers of the setting sun, so too sank my hopes for a daytime exchange. Just when we were beginning to doubt our actions The Terrible Tango signaled a text. It was the kidnapper. I read it out to the team ... *6043 National Road, Mabini. Money must be in account by 8 P.M., come alone. MK.* We studied each other for a moment contemplating the message.

I checked my watch and asked, "It's six o'clock, is that enough time to get there?"

"Yes, luckily we're close. It's only fifteen minutes from here," Dan said.

"And the money?" I prompted.

"I will need to send a text to my bank manager. The funds will then be transferred immediately," Nick responded.

"Right. I'll notify the Lovejoy's, then we'll devise an assault plan."

"Okay, I'll assemble the troops," Dan rumbled.

I went outside to get a better signal and phoned Lola. I told her we were getting set to go in. There wasn't much else I could say. It felt awkward, both of us aware of the consequences of failure. With a tremble of emotion in her voice, she wished me the best of luck.

I went back inside where Nick, Dan and his three troopers, dressed in night camouflage military fatigues with matching painted faces, were waiting. I felt out of synch dressed in black jeans, my favorite T, and Nike black/hyper punch/photo blue/anthracite trainers, but hey, I guess it was my show after all and I could dress how I wanted.

We carried out weapon checks, and then Dan displayed a topographical map of the area on his laptop.

"This is the target ... we will use the Pajero along the long driveway up to the house until here," he said gruffly. "Then we will deploy and go in on foot ... Nick will accompany Axis to the house."

He changed the picture to a satellite image.

"This photo was taken fifteen minutes ago. As you can see, there is no life to be seen anywhere. He triggered an infrared filter and six stationary figures appeared in red.

"Can't see what's inside the house, but note the hostiles holed up around it ... they will be our targets.

"How should we play this Nick?" I asked.

"I will hide under a thermo blanket in the rear of

the Pajero, to avoid detection. Once you're inside the house, I'll find a way to follow you in."

"The kidnapper will be set up to detonate the bomb by cell-phone. Theoretically, he will be a distance away but with the house in sight, or positioned for a relayed message. We expect he will wait until he has the money and for Axis to be inside, before he detonates the bomb," Dan said matter-of-factly.

"So I will let it go down to the wire before I transfer the money," Nick said.

"Exactly Nick. Meantime we will knock over his support hand to hand. It will be risky, they will have orders to signal the kidnapper at the first sign of trouble," Dan said. He had an excited expression – he obviously enjoyed his gig. He'd made it perfectly clear how tough it was going to be. The thought of being blown to bits gave me nausea.

"Will you be able to handle this Stone?" Dan asked.

The question put me on the spot – my Aussie bravado kicked in – I gulped, "Yeah, too late to chicken out now."

"It is not now that I am worried about Stone … it is when you see Kitty sitting on a time bomb. That is when you will have the weird feeling of having to make a decision that could well end your own life."

I could see what he was getting at and it wasn't pretty.

"I can hack it," I said, with a fake smirk of confidence.

"Any questions?" Dan eyed us, but there were none.

~~~

The butterflies were a-flutter in my stomach by the time Nick and the others were under cover in the car making it look like I was alone. I gave a running commentary all the way there and was just beginning to relax when Dan spoke up from behind me.

"The driveway entrance should be up ahead on your left."

"Roger that," I replied getting into the lingo.

The rolling hills descended in a series of sweeping curves until they reached Balayan Bay, maybe a couple of clicks away. In the middle distance perched on top of a hill was the house with the driveway snaking up to it. The gaunt turrets and spires of the house made a sinister silhouette against the night sky like the opening shot of a horror movie.

"Got it, I'm turning into the driveway," I reported.

"Pull up when you can get under tree cover. Get out, walk into the headlights and check the map in them," Dan ordered.

Navigating the narrow dark driveway was tricky. A full moon was rising out of the Bay and that added to the eeriness. I stopped the Pajero under a big tree, hopped out and acted as ordered. While I created the distraction Dan and his men silently debarked and coalesced into the darkness.

I looked up. The old, two-story Spanish hacienda with its red terracotta tiled roof, stood out in the moonlight like a sore thumb. There were no lights burning inside. With the charade over and the troops deployed, I climbed back into the Pajero and drove up to the forecourt of the old house. As I stepped out of the car I felt for the security of my pistol ... a weapon tends to calm the nerves somewhat.

The kidnapper had chosen the location well, it was isolated, run down and neglected – it looked like no one had lived there for decades. He could do what he liked with it. The tropical trees surrounding the house cast sinister shadows in the moonlight.

I went up to the decayed front door that was slightly ajar. Now came the tough part – where is she? I stepped inside the dark entrance and scanned for signs of life. It was more dilapidated inside than out. A once regal wooden balustrade leading to the second floor had been all but stripped of its timber long ago. Moonlight beamed down through broken tiles in the roof highlighting gaping holes in the floor where the floorboards had been swiped. Just another hazard I'd have to negotiate in the darkness. I heard a "psst" from behind. It was from Nick ... his camouflage was so good that at twenty feet away he was only a ghostly apparition. It was comforting to know he was there to back me up. He threw me a penlight, which allowed me to move on with more confidence. Stepping over chasms that I figured descended to the basement, I noticed recent drag marks and footprints in the dusty floor. The tracks led through a pair of rickety doors barely hanging from rusted hinges to what looked to be a dining room. I followed the tracks and at the doors carefully prized open the sturdiest one ... it creaked and groaned in protest but let me through. Inside the room I stopped dead in my tracks careful not to swallow too hard because my heart was in my throat.

In the middle of the room bathed in a pool of moonlight streaming down in a ribbon from a break in the ceiling two-floors above, stood an old wooden chair and in it was a naked female – Kitty. She was blindfolded, unconscious with her chin resting on her chest. Her arms had been tied behind the chair and her ankles fastened to the rear legs. Dan had it right, as soon as I caught sight of the bomb under the chair my nerves kicked in big time. The penlight flickered in my shaky hand when I tried to scan the rest of the room. It flashed on two cameras up high and I froze, pocketed the light and stayed put in the doorway. Something touched me on the shoulder and I jumped with fright.

"Ugh shit!" I gasped.

"It's only me, you all right?" Nick whispered.

"Yeah, two cameras ... ten o'clock and two ... we're out of shot here. Are you set to make the transfer?"

"I see them," he said and produced a device.

"What's that?" I queried.

"A G5 cellular phone jammer ... it has a radius of twenty meters. It will buy us a thirty-second window.

"Window? What window? Explain please?"

He produced a knife.

"I will cut her free, you pick her up and hightail it out of here with her."

Carrying a limp body all that way didn't sound sensible for a guy like me whose idea of exercise is to walk once in a while instead of riding the elevator.

"You've got to be kidding man!" I protested. "They'll be cleaning us off the walls with a fucking mop?" I growled.

"Maybe, maybe not ... follow me."

Chapter Fifteen

He didn't give me time to debate it any further and just took off like a rocket. When he got to her, he dropped the jammer beside the chair and immediately began hacking away at the ropes binding her wrists to it. I raced over beside him puffing like I'd just run a marathon, hastily slipped my arm around the back between her and the back of the chair, and took her weight on my shoulder. With her hands free she slumped against me. Nick knelt down behind her and started on her ankle binds. I tensed up ready to take all of her weight. Her long red hair wafted around my face and smelt good, her skin felt smooth, she had lovely breasts ... I scolded myself for thinking about her nudity ... though it did add a little spice to the moment, one thing, I didn't notice any obvious signs of abuse on her body. Bloody-hell, I was earning my fee on this one. I hoped the seconds weren't counting down as fast as my heart was thumping.

"Go!" Nick suddenly cried out.

I quickly slid my free hand under her legs and lifted her in my arms like a baby – a very heavy baby – and then I took off as fast as my legs could carry me. Nick was close behind I could hear his footsteps drumming loudly on the wooden floor.

Without the help of the penlight I had no idea where the cavities were in the floor, I got through the doorway and suddenly felt my left legs go from under me. I'd gone through a bloody great hole in the floor. We stopped with an agonizing jolt ... my arms and Kitty legs preventing us falling completely through. I don't know how but I managed to hang on to her. It felt like I'd popped both my shoulders from the impact. Lucky she was unconscious, if she'd been awake and rigid, we would have ended up in the basement for sure. Nick appeared, and as he lifted us out of the cavity, there was an almighty explosion. Just as I drew my legs out of the hole the shockwave hit me with a force that sent me sliding across the floor on my backside – it was like the hand of God had given me one almighty shove. My ears were ringing like Church bells. Kitty was no longer in my arms. I looked up and immediately ducked down flat on the floorboards to get under a massive fireball that roared out of the living room and passed overhead. Instinctively, I curled up into a fetal position knowing there was more coming. And I was right – a wind hit me hard carrying with it a salvo of debris. When I felt the explosion had passed, I blinked my eyes open and sat up wondering how much of me was left. The air was thick with dust. The lounge room was ablaze in thick orange flames. I could just make out two dark figures sprawled out on the floor not moving. Suddenly, hands appeared out the smoke and lifted me up by the arms. I was carried at speed out through the front door – it was surreal, I thought it must have been angels extracting me from the fires of hades. No, wait, why would they do that? I'm agnostic ... that would mean ... oh dear, maybe this was proof of divinity. Is it an out of body experience? I hope so ... if I live, I can write the book. Where's the bright light? Then I saw it. There *was* light at the end of the tunnel! It passed only to be replaced by another, then another. I squinted to focus and recognized oyster light fittings and realized I was on my back looking up at lights flitting past. My hearing returned some and I could hear squeaking and rolling sounds – I realized I was on a hospital trolley being wheeled at speed along a corridor. I sat bolt upright ... and then darkness consumed me.

Voices ... I opened my eyes alerted by them ... one

sounded familiar ... it was Cortez. He saw I was awake and leaned over my hospital bed to speak.

"How do you feel Stone?"

"Like something the cat dragged in," I groaned through parched lips. "Where am I?"

"Makati med, you were injured in your rescue mission."

I tried to move but my shoulders ached like hell.

"And the others?"

"Vargas is in a private suite upstairs ... naturally. Kitty is with him. She's on life support ... he has superficial injuries like yours."

"Will she be all right?"

"It's touch and go, she took some shrapnel."

"I'm surprised we even survived it."

"You were lucky to have Ilagan and his men to get you out. Apparently, the house burnt down very quickly."

I counted the lumps in my bed.

"Am I all here?"

"You took some splinters in the right arm ... but you'll live. You can get up if you like."

It felt stupid being in a hospital bed for an injury so minor and so I struggled up.

"Your clothes are in the closet," he said.

I opened it and was disappointed to find my best T-shirt torn to shreds.

"Damn!" I complained as I stripped off the hospital gown and pulled on my jeans, then I put on what was left of the T. I picked up my gun.

"You don't have a permit for that."

"So? Call the police," I joked.

I went into the en-suite bathroom and splashed water on my face. Checked the mirror, there were small lacerations all over my face and my forearms. I found a toothbrush and paste, so used them.

"Just how bad are they?" I called out to Sancho who was still sitting on the edge of the bed.

"Vargas is up and about ... like you only minor cuts and bruises but the girl took a nasty hit ... some flying debris hit her in the head and peppered her body ... no clothes to protect her either. You should have told me you were going to make the exchange."

I came out and eyeballed him. "Sancho, I couldn't take the risk ... I was acting on instructions from the family, you know that."

That riled him up. He jumped off the bed, pointed his finger threateningly and shouted, "Just who gave you permission to go on a rampage around the countryside like a vigilante death squad trying to rescue a damsel in distress?"

I returned serve with verve, "Nick Vargas and his two million bucks that's who! Let's get something straight here Chief Inspector ... the most likely suspect in the kidnapping of Kitty Lovejoy and the murder of Chicki Dee is an untouchable cop, one of yours. So the real question is: with only hours before the ransom deadline would you have risked saving Kitty's life by informing cops with such dubious integrity, all the details?"

"No. I expect you might be right Stone, but after what happened, I think you have only created a bigger and more threatening problem than you originally had."

"And why would that be, we've got the victim back for Christ's sake?"

"Because Vargas didn't pay the ransom and the kidnapper failed to kill you and Kitty ... so she is still a target for whatever it is she knows and you for what you might find out."

"Oh shit!" I gasped wide-eyed.

I needed to pay Nick a visit to unload on him. We rode the elevator together to the ninth floor

Presidential suites, where Sancho led the way along a long narrow corridor. Two uniforms posted outside the door singled out the correct room. A nod from Sancho gained us entry.

It was a fancy set up, more like a hotel penthouse than a hospital room ... reserved for the rich – obviously. Nick was sitting in an armchair dressed in casual attire, reading a newspaper, a dozen or so plasters decorating his face, neck and hands.

He lowered the paper and raised an eyebrow at me.

"You obviously know by now that I didn't pay the ransom and you're pissed, right?"

"You're damn right I'm pissed. Nice to see you too Nick," I added with as much cynicism as I could muster.

His face exhibited similar bomb residue to mine. I sat down opposite him.

"You of course chose not to tell me because you preferred to risk my life than be up front."

"I wasn't sure you would understand. Winston Lovejoy came up with the idea."

"What ... good for him ... and so that makes it right does it? Fucked up the ass without even feeling a thing. Good to know who you can trust." I stood. "Well that puts an end to this job, it's time for me to present an invoice and get out of Dodge. Goodbye Nick, nice knowing you." I got up and then stormed out of the room.

Sancho gave chase and stopped me in the corridor.

"Stone! Wait. You can't quit now my friend, the job is only half done. We still have to catch the bastard or he will get away with it."

I turned and got in his face. "So now I'm your friend. Look, it isn't my problem any more pal."

"But what if Kitty dies? What about Chicki Dee?"

"Man, one minute you're reprimanding me for breaking police protocol and the next you're pleading with me to stay on the case. What is it with you Filipinos, you don't trust anyone ... including each other?"

"I guess it looks like I am in two minds my friend, but if you are right and Cruz is behind this then it will take the three of us to nail him."

"I don't know, Vargas could've got me killed. He used me and I don't dig that."

"He also saved your life." He said resting a consoling hand on my shoulder. "He was only doing what he could to save Kitty. You would probably have done the same thing yourself ... wouldn't you?"

"Yeah maybe," I reluctantly agreed.

"Look, you have every right to go back home and leave the case with us my friend, but I think you have more integrity than that. I know using that word sounds weird coming from a Filipino cop, but we're not all bent. Some of us have pride in what we do."

"I didn't realize you had a sense of humor."

"Only when I laugh," he said, his gold tooth glimmering in his smile.

He'd convinced me to bat on, but we needed to put together a fresh strategy, so we went back to consult Nick. Sancho made it clear he believed the kidnapper would make a move to kill Kitty when he discovers she survived the bomb and that the same would apply to me. It would be easier to keep Kitty a secret than me. My answer to that was to use me as bait to lure him in but Sancho wouldn't agree.

"It is far too easy to have someone hit in the Philippines," he said sternly. "All a bent cop needs to do is have a jailed killer released from prison for a couple of hours for a hit in exchange for money or favors."

"Yeah, I guess so," I allowed.

"A hit only costs five thousand pesos Axis," Nick

added.

"A hundred bucks! Fuck, life is cheap here, no wonder it's tough for you cops."

"If you saw our pay packet you would be shocked."

"He would get less than two hundred bucks a week," Nick said referring to Sancho.

"That's probably the gas allowance for an Aussie senior investigator," I submitted. "But I still reckon I'd make an ideal bait."

We agreed to sleep on it and then meet up again to discuss a new plan. In the meantime I was warned to watch my ass and not trust anybody – after what had just happened that sounded a bit hypocritical.

Chapter Sixteen

When I got back to the Shang, I needed to call Lola. I was pissed that Winston had made a sly deal with Nick and put me in danger, so I rang them to dump my shit and was surprised when Winston answered the phone.

"Winston, Stone here ... just the man I wanted to speak to ... Kitty? She's in intensive care, why ask me how she is, seems you've got a tighter bond with Vargas? Listen to me, the lousy fee you're paying me doesn't include getting blown to bits ... no that doesn't come with the job ... staying alive does ... I resent being used, especially by my own client. I'll tell you what I mean ... you did a bloody side deal with Vargas not to pay the ransom and I should have been told about it. Sure, I still would've gone in. Anyhow, that's ancient history, make me a better deal or I'm out of here. Yes, okay, that sounds reasonable ..." Appeased I changed my tone. "I want half in my account ASAP and the rest on completion. Good. Incidentally, why did you answer Lola's phone? She's what?"

Still choking on the news from old man Lovejoy, I grabbed a towel and went down for a mid afternoon dip in the pool.

I phoned Ricky from poolside and was glad to hear he'd recovered enough to return to the case. We arranged to meet in the morning for breakfast by the pool. There was little to keep me at poolside that time of day, all the talent was strutting its stuff to Makati's trendiest bars for happy hour. I went back to my room to shower and just stepped out when the door buzzer sounded. I went into the bedroom, pulled on a robe, collected the thirty-eight from the top drawer of the bedroom bureau, and slipped it into the side pocket that sagged a little under the weight. What the hell? I figured I preferred to be sartorially dead than the real thing. Then I went to the door, and feeling real brave, opened it a couple of inches. Standing there resplendent in a little black Chanel number was beautiful Lola.

"Did I get you out of bed?" She queried.

"No, only the shower," I smiled. "Come in."

Her dark eyes smoldered a little while she cased the room expecting to find a naked babe.

"Let me make you a drink," I said.

"I'd like that." She gave me a long look of appraisal. "Is all that hair on your chest for real, Axis?"

"It has to go back in the morning," I said. "I get a reduced rate for nightly rentals from a little old wigmaker who grows mushrooms in the hotel basement. "

I made for the bar fridge and mixed a couple of drinks.

"Hope you like rye." I handed her one, then sat in an armchair and raised my glass to her. "Cheers. Welcome to Manila."

She sat opposite on the couch, crossed her shapely legs and offered her glass.

"Thanks, cheers big ears."

"All the better to hear you with," I scoffed.

"So how's Kitty?"

"Ask your buddy Nick?"

"Why?"

"Because you and Winston sold me out."

"What are you saying?"

"You had me risk my life by not paying the ransom and Nick not telling me. That's no way to treat your beloved colleague. More like an enemy," I remonstrated.

"That wasn't any of my doing, I knew nothing about it ... I would never ..."

"Don't sell me any bullshit lady."

She got up and cruised over to me catlike as if on a cloud and then slid onto my lap. She pouched her ruby red lips, gently pressed them against mine and then eyeballed me up close – real close.

"I wouldn't get you hurt ... honest," she purred.

Then she kissed me. I didn't need any further encouragement than that. It took me only a matter of seconds to whip her into the bedroom, undress her, slip out of my clothes, my organ rampant and raging to go. I reached for her, crushing her soft, pliant body in my arms and forcing her legs apart with my own. We struggled and squirmed on the bed. Our need was urgent. We rolled from one side of the bed to the other clamped in a tight embrace, our mouths pressed together, hands and tongues probing, exploring. She extricated herself from me, and easing me onto my back, took hold of my twitching, demanding rod and lowered her lips to it. She was an expert, and her tongue was everywhere, laving my tingling flesh, bringing me almost to the point where I felt I could hold on no longer and I had to exert all my will to hold back the rush. Finally, I pushed her head out between my legs, and turning her onto her back, brought myself up and straddled her, my hands pushing the backs of her thighs right up so that her legs were on my shoulders as I thrust myself into her. The movement was fluid and easy as I penetrated her, the whole length of my rod sliding effortlessly into the warm, moist sheath. She fitted me like a glove. Her head rolled from side to side on the pillow beneath me as my body pounded into her, her vaginal muscles contracting and gripping me tight as my weapon thrust into her deeply. Her moans became more frantic and high-pitched. Her fingernails raked my back. My heart was thumping wildly and with one massive lunge, her rigid body arched from the bed to meet me, we came to a simultaneous shuddering climax that left us both spent and gasping for breath.

~~~

In the morning, I climbed out of bed and, hastily throwing on my clothes, finished my own drink in two gulps and hers in three. The kidnapper would know by now that Kitty Lovejoy had been rescued and was in a coma at a private hospital. That would attract him like a moth to a flame. It was time to make the next move. I quickly penned a note telling Lola to stay put in the room. It was critical to keep her presence in Manila a secret, as she could easily become a secondary target for the kidnapper. I said I'd call her in the room at 10 A.M., and then rode the elevator down to meet Ricky at poolside.

He was waiting when I got there. It was humid, felt like a storm was coming.

"Hey Ricky, good to see you back on deck."

"Thanks boss ... I heard on the news about the rescue and Miss Kitty in a coma. You look like you took some shrapnel. He will still come to get her you know. Probably send somebody else. Did he get the ransom?"

"No."

"Why? What happened?"

"At the last minute the family chose not to pay," I growled.

"Then you better watch your back boss, the kidnapper will blame you for that."

"Other than retribution and being out of pocket, what do you think is driving this bloke?"

"I think Kitty must know something incriminating. Maybe she saw his face ... knows him even. Or maybe she knows something about the murder of Pablo

Cortez."

"Yeah, well she did spend time with Ringo Raye, so there is no telling what she knows. Boy it's muggy."

"There's a typhoon coming."

"When?"

"It will probably hit tonight ... it's a big one. Have you been in a typhoon before?"

"We get southerly busters in Sydney and the odd tornado but as I understand it they are nothing compared to what you guys get here."

"So it will be a new experience for you."

"One I could do without Ricky, we've got enough on our plate without worrying about bloody Mother Nature."

I checked my watch. "Okay, let's order up ... we need to be at the hospital in two hours. Can you drive?"

He held up the plaster cast on his right hand. "Lucky I am left-handed. No worries boss."

After we'd indulged ourselves on an assortment of Shangri-La culinary delights and copious cups of freshly brewed coffee, we were caffeine wired and hot to trot. My phone vibrated ... it was Cortez.

"Sancho, what's up?"

"A short while I ago received a phone call from the office of the Mayor of Makati," he said with a solemn tone.

"Okay ... and?"

"His office was asking about you."

"Me?" I said surprised. "I didn't know I was so popular."

"It's my guess you will soon get a call from Mayor Rodriguez."

"Hmm, this is not sounding good."

"I would say someone has pulled some strings from up high to stop the investigation now that you have Kitty back."

"Has he shut you down?"

"You could say that. But you are regarded as the loose cannon my friend."

"Yes, I can understand that ... you can be shut down but I can't."

"Yes, that is it exactly."

"What's your advice Sancho?"

"My investigation into the murder of Chicki Dee can't be shut down, it is ongoing, but they know it is a road to nowhere. I have been reminded that Kitty Lovejoy is a foreigner and that finding her kidnapper isn't a priority."

"That smacks of it becoming a racist cold case."

"Sure does," he said dispiritedly.

"So tell me Sancho, does this Mayor Rodriguez have the capacity to run me out of town?"

"Absolutely," he said emphatically.

"And you can't help me?"

"Only if you want to spend time in a prison cell."

"No thanks it's not my favorite smell! So either I talk to this guy or avoid him?"

"That decision is yours my friend but my advice is to talk to him. I don't want you run out of town ... as I see it you are the best chance we've got of rounding up these criminals."

"Hey, flattery will get you everywhere," I said perkily.

"How is Ricky?" He asked.

"He's right here with me back on the case."

"Good, then ask him about Rodriguez, he knows a lot about him."

"Okay will do. Talk later."

I hung up and gazed over my sunglasses at Ricky sitting opposite me.

"Did you get the drift of that conversation?"

"Yes, you're to expect a call from Mayor Rodriguez

and Cortez has been shut down, the case has gone cold."

"You've got it in one. So tell me about this dude."

"Okay boss, before I joined the force I worked for him in security. He was running for mayor of Ermita back then."

"When was this?" I asked.

"The end of eighties, back then Ermita was like P. Burgos is today but with many more girlie bars. Rodriguez got voted in mayor because he promised to get rid of the bars. I was part of the task force to close them down."

"Sounds a tough gig."

"It was very tough ... mainly because the fifty or so bars were operated by foreigners, Australians, Americans, a couple from the Netherlands. They were all gangsters in one form or another – it was serious prostitution – lots of money being made from the heavy traffic of American military personnel, tourists and lots of rig pigs from offshore oilrigs on furlough. Anyhow to cut a long story short it turned into a street war ... and we were on the losing side. That's when Rodriguez pulled his trump card: the bar owners didn't own the freehold to their bars, they only leased the premises from Filipinos. Rodriguez got to each and every property owner, bought the properties from them and then evicted the bar owners. It was all done quickly before they could even realize what was happening and by the time they did it was all too late."

"He's got guts ... that wouldn't have gone down too well."

"He was only saved from being hit because he cut a deal with the biggest bar owners to move to P. Burgos Street in Makati, where they still are today. Rodriguez then developed the Ermita properties and made millions. The irony is that two years ago he was voted mayor of Makati but hasn't tried to clean up the prostitution in P. Burgos Street, like he did in Ermita, they say because of the deal he'd struck."

"He sold his soul to the devil huh? Do you think that deal was with Ringo Raye?"

"Raye didn't have a bar in Ermita, but he bought into P. Burgos Street at the very same time Rodriguez became mayor of Makati."

"What a coincidence."

"Many believe way too much of a coincidence."

"So let's assume he's in bed with Raye, he might also be in bed with Cruz?"

"That's very possible because he and Cruz were amigos back in the Ermita days, and many people wondered how Rodriguez got the money to buy out all of those properties."

"Could have been drug money from Cruz."

"A big chance I reckon."

"So Ricky, how should I deal with this guy when he rings?"

"Very, very carefully boss, he is not a man to be messed with ... he is more dangerous than Raye and Cruz put together."

"I hear you ... You know an old friend of mine in the force once taught me that buying time on a case is good, it makes the bad guys sweat," I held up my smartphone and turned it off. "There, I'll talk to him when I'm good and ready. In the meantime we've got a job to do."

Chapter Seventeen

The valet delivered Ricky's Corolla to the Shang forecourt and we hopped in.

"Where are we going boss?"

"St. Luke's in Quezon City."

The traffic on EDSA Boulevard was fearful, so I kicked back in the seat to catch forty winks. Ricky woke me twenty minutes later.

"Boss, there's a bike tailing us and I don't like it."

I quickly sat up in the seat and positioned the passenger side mirror for better view behind. Sure enough a Yamaha FZ16 was right on our hammer.

"Can you lose him Ricky?"

"Not in this traffic boss."

"Are you certain he's trouble?"

"Just my instincts tell me. I'll turn into the next street and see if he follows.

"Good idea."

Ricky hit the blinkers and took the next street on the right. We both checked the rear vision mirrors.

"He is following us," Ricky said dolefully.

I sighted a gas station up ahead.

"Ricky, drive into that gas station and out the other side then head back the way we were coming."

Ricky got the idea and drove slowly up to a bowser. The biker followed. Once the bike had stopped Ricky put his foot down and we screeched out onto the road. He did a high-speed turn and powered back toward Ortigas leaving the bike in our wake. When we reached Ortigas, Ricky pushed into the line of traffic. I checked behind – the biker was about six cars back and had pulled out to pass them to catch us.

"He's coming," I warned Ricky. I pulled my gun

and held it in my lap at the ready. "Damn it! We'll have to take him on. Can you handle it?"

"Not much choice is there boss?

"No, okay, turn into the next side street and stop."

I braced myself ready to shoot him when he pulled up beside us.

Ricky turned off Ortigas into Frontera Drive, and stopped.

"He's coming fast!" Ricky shrieked. "Get down!"

The bike screamed up on my side of the car – I wasn't expecting that, I figured it would be the driver's side ... it all happened in slow motion – I ducked – he emptied the clip into the car. Head down I shielded my face from the shower of glass from the shattering windows. I huddled as low in the seat as I could hoping he wasn't reloading and then came up to take a shot at him ... I was too late ... the bike sped off. Ricky was in the driver's side well ... I patted him on the head.

"You can come up now mate, he's gone."

But Ricky didn't move. I looked at the palm of my hand ... it was smeared with blood ... Ricky had taken a head shot – he was dead. In shock I pulled my phone, turned it back on and phoned Cortez. I don't even know what I said but within half an hour a team arrived with blue strobe lights flashing and sirens sounding. The chaos of them arriving brought me back to reality and I realized I was sitting on the curb beside the bullet peppered Corolla in a daze, traumatized by the attack and the loss of my friend.

Sancho led me over to his black Nissan X-trail, sat me on the back seat and put a flask of brandy in my shaking hand. I took a big swig, and then sank down and put my head in my hands. Sancho placed a consoling hand on my shoulder ... everything we were doing suddenly felt futile. I was responsible for Ricky and Chicki, they were good people and didn't deserve to be killed by these bastards. At a time like this I questioned everything I was doing – was it worth it?

"What can I say Axis, this is Manila," Sancho said in sympathy. "This was always going to happen. Did you speak with Rodriguez?"

"No, I turned my phone off, I'll speak with him when I'm good and ready."

"That might have been a bad move Axis."

I got the inference and hated it.

On the way to St. Luke's with Cortez, I phoned Lola and told her what had happened. The news freaked her out. She agreed to stay put and to stay vigilant but she was scared – really scared. The scary thing for me was that there had been no missed call: Rodriguez hadn't phoned – meaning Ricky's murder was probably a warning from him. Cortez certainly seemed to think that was the case.

The plan was to use the suite at St. Luke's as a ruse to ensnare the kidnapper. All the while Kitty was secretly on life support at Makati Medical Hospital. Nick and I would take up armed vigilance at St. Luke's. We expected the kidnapper to believe Kitty was hospitalized there after we'd issued a false news report to all media. By the hit on Ricky the ruse had worked, but it had cost him his life.

We rode the elevator up to the private suites top floor of Tower One, then entered past the two uniforms posted outside the room. We found Nick on the phone. He quickly terminated the call and jumped up from the armchair when he saw my face and the blood spatter on my jacket.

"Axis! What the hell!" He exclaimed.

We filled him in on what had happened including the story on Rodriguez. He slumped into an armchair with his head in hands.

"These assholes are getting the better of us," he

groaned.

"My actions have cost another life," I said.

"I'm sorry you lost your friend, Axis," Nick said sincerely.

Losing Ricky hurt deep down in my guts and I could feel the bile of reprisal rising. My mission had now taken on a new face: I wasn't going to rest until I got the bastards that killed my friend. Ricky had taken a fatal bullet for me – I owe him to get square.

"I can feel your angst Axis and I sympathize with you but you can't let it blind you," Nick said compassionately.

"Don't worry Axis you will get your shot at getting even," Sancho said in a manner that felt like he'd made the same speech before. I nodded slowly and eyeballed him.

"I hear you Sancho," I said knowing that hard cold hate had seized my purpose.

Just as Sancho was leaving, he got a call from a doctor at Makati Med ... it was good news ... Kitty was out of the coma. The news radically changed our plans.

"Does the hit on Ricky reopen the case Sancho?" I asked sternly.

"It does," he growled.

~~~

It was imperative to talk with Kitty to establish what she might know to make her a target. Sancho drove us to Makati Med at break-neck speed with lights a-flashing and the siren sounding. On the way, we swung by the Shang and collected Lola. Heavily disguised she slipped surreptitiously into the car at a secure exit reserved only for dignitaries and celebrities intent on escaping the press and fans. The same applied when we arrived at Makati Med: the security was tight, as there was plenty at stake.

A nurse led us past two uniformed sentries into the

Presidential suite, where we found Kitty in bed. This was the first time for me to see her conscious. Lola flew across the room and embraced her sister. Looking at them together, I realized how much alike they were ... almost identical except for the hair color: Lola blonde, Kitty red.

The three of us gave the sisters a moment then, it was Nick's turn. With the emotional stuff out of the way, it was time to ask Kitty some pertinent questions.

Her lack of make-up heightened the pallor of her face. Her eyes were red-rimmed and swollen, her lips were parched but there was a twinkle in her eyes that said she was in control. I sat on the edge of the bed and looked into her bloodshot eyes.

"Kitty, I'm Axis Stone, a private investigator from Sydney ... I've been working on your kidnapping."

"Yeah they told me you carried me out of the explosion. You risked your life for me," she said in a croaky voice and a pain-ridden smile. "I can't thank you enough."

She took my hand and I could feel from her grip she was still very weak.

"I know you need rest but it's important to ask you some questions. Can you handle it?"

With tears welling in her eyes, she nodded affirmative.

"Did you see the face of your kidnapper or anyone connected?"

She shook her head.

"What about when you were handed a phone to speak with your family?"

"No, I was blindfolded."

"Okay, is there anything you can tell me to help us identify your kidnappers or where you were being held?"

She shut her eyes tight to think while tears

squeezed their way through her pressed lids. Her face grimaced with pain. I wasn't sure if it was from the pain of her wounds or the memory of how she'd been treated by her kidnappers. Suddenly her eyes opened.

"Gum, my gum," she said excitedly.

"Gum?"

"Most of the time I was on a boat, I could hear lapping water, birds ..." she coughed. "I could also hear footsteps drumming above me. I was kept naked, blindfolded, drugged ... it's all a blur."

"You said your gum?"

"When they nabbed me they shot me full of smack or something. I woke up tied in a chair, blindfolded and naked. I could feel the air tingling on my skin ... I still had my chewing gum in my mouth."

I heard Lola snigger affectionately behind me ... chewing gum must have been one of Kitty's traits.

"A guy arrived and took me into a tiny toilet to pee. I took the gum out and stuck it under the seat. It would still be there. From then on, the same guy brought me a bucket and I figure watched me go. He also washed me down with a sponge ... had a great time, if you know what I mean. By then I knew him by his strong body odor."

"Did they feed you?" Lola asked.

"Same guy spoon-fed me. Never spoke. To be honest I don't know what he got up to with me. He'd jab me when he was finished ... I was out of it all the time ... that's why it's all such a blur."

Just as I was about to ask her why she's a target — a nurse thundered into the room and ordered us out in no uncertain terms. Kitty was to rest and believe me this nurse who was obviously a former SS Nazi officer under Heinrich Himmler, wasn't to be messed with ... we acquiesced and headed back to my hotel to discuss the next move.

~~~

There were four of us in my room and it was obvious Nick was totally besotted by Lola. She was after all the spitting image of Kitty, and in my humble biased opinion, sexier.

"I guess we abandon the St. Luke's entrapment and go for the chewing gum," I proposed.

"We will have to send the gum to Australia for DNA analysis."

"That won't matter Sancho, all we need do is find the gum under the toilet seat in the boat to implicate the owner," I countered.

"Well that means we have three boats to search at Subic marina," Nick advanced.

"Will we need a search warrant Sancho?" I asked, hoping not.

He rubbed his furrowed brow with a look of anguish on his craggy face.

"If I apply for a warrant and the kidnapper is who we think he is, Cruz, he will find out and ..."

"The boat will just sail into the setting sun," Nick finished for him.

"That doesn't leave us much choice or time," I submitted.

"It sounds extremely dangerous to me," Lola said with genuine concern.

It felt like a lay down misère to me. From the inception there had been something suspicious about Ringo's boat.

"My money is on Raye's boat Bodyshot," I announced confidently. "Who's up for a drink?"

We got stuck into the bar fridge, fortunately it had been restocked while we were out. There wasn't much left by the time we'd finished but at least we had a plan. At 3 p.m., Nick would have Dan chopper us up to Subic for the three of us to raid the boats. Sancho wouldn't join us because it had to be an unsanctioned invasion. If we got the chewing gum evidence from Bodyshot, we were to call Sancho who would be on standby to raid Ringo's apartment and arrest him for suspected kidnapping under article 267 of Philippine law.

Chapter Eighteen

I saw Nick and Sancho out and then turned my attention to Lola.

"It's after lunchtime, I feel like something to eat. You hungry?"

Reclining on the sofa, she fired me a devilish grin and then gently lifted the front of her skirt exposing her smoothly shaven cleave.

"How about an appetizer?" She purred.

I didn't need any more of an invitation than that ... any girl who doesn't wear knickers gets my vote.

After she'd swallowed her 10 cc appetizer, I rang room service and ordered a feast – champagne and the works. If this was going to be my last supper then it was going to be in style. We were on the profiteroles in chocolate sauce, when The Terrible Tango sounded. Speak of the devil – it was Raye.

"Ringo," I said loud so that Lola knew who it was.

"Stone, haven't heard from you in a while, thought you might be dead."

"Not if I have anything to do with it."

"Heard you got Kitty back but she's in a coma. What's the prognosis?"

"Could be days or weeks before she comes out of it, no one knows. Tell me something, do you know Vic Cruz?"

"Cruz you say, don't know ... name rings a bell."

"Yeah, I can hear it chiming from here."

"What's that supposed to mean?"

"Not a lot but the name keeps cropping up."

"Yeah, in relation to what?"

"Um, drugs, murder, kidnapping, you know, that sort of thing," I said casually.

"Can't help you Stone, I've told you that before."

I could tell by his tone he wasn't going any further.

"Ricky Esposo got hit this morning, have you heard?" I asked the leading question.

"No, are you telling me he's dead?"

"A shooter on a bike tried to take us out and Ricky got hit," I said angrily.

"I'm sorry to hear that."

"Tell me about Rodriguez?"

"Who?"

"The mayor."

"What's he got to do with this?"

"That's what I'm trying to find out."

"So where is Kitty, I'd like to pay her a visit," he said changing the subject.

"Like I said, she hasn't got much to say at the moment, but when she does, I promise you'll be one of the first to know."

"That sounds sarcastic Stone, you've got yourself an attitude problem or am I just imagining it?"

"Comes with the gig."

"Yours or mine?"

"Probably both."

"Was the ransom paid?" He asked.

"No, so that's fifteen love to the good guys."

"Watch your serve Stone ... Catch you round."

He didn't seem very pleased with my rhetoric and terminated the call. I didn't mind, my aim was to put him on notice.

"I can tell by your body language that was intimidating," Lola said.

"Kitty's ex and big time local gangster ... Ringo Raye ... it's his boat we're going to hit tonight. If we find what we're after, he'll be facing life for kidnapping."

"What makes you think he'll stay in town after what you just told him?"

"When I mentioned Cruz and Rodriguez, he knew it was checkmate. Now he's only got two options left ... run or fight ... and knowing him ... he'll fight."

"Are you saying he'll try and kill you and Kitty?"

"He already tried this morning and poor Ricky took the bullet."

"Was that him? I thought it was the other guy the mayor?" She shrieked.

"They're all in it together, Raye, Rodriguez and Cruz. None of them personally the shooter, but one of them sure as eggs arranged it."

"I'm confused ... and that doesn't make me feel very secure with all of this."

I gave her a big hug.

"We have to try and stay one step ahead of these bastards, kid."

She stared deep into my eyes and I watched the tears welling up.

"Is Kitty safe where she is?"

"Safer than us, we'll keep the deception going that she's at St. Luke's, just as an added precaution."

I checked my timepiece.

"It's time to go," I said, and then kissed her passionately.

"Please don't get yourself killed," she whimpered in our clinch.

"I don't have time for that," I chuckled jokingly. Deep down inside I knew she was right – this could all end nasty. "Don't go anywhere and don't answer the phone, okay?"

She nodded. I could see the fear in her eyes.

~~~

It took only a few minutes to hightail it across Ayala to the Peninsula Hotel, and then up to the helipad on the roof. I stood there taking in the view of the city at sunset. There were huge thunderheads building up in the south I guessed the typhoon Ricky told me was due. Soon enough a chopper appeared in the darkening sky.

Ten minutes later, I was in the backseat next to Nick, looking down on Manila Bay four thousand feet below. We headed north by northwest to Subic Bay. We didn't talk ... there was a disconsolate mood ... like we were on a special services mission, unlikely to return. Makes sense to feel that way after the loss of Ricky and the screw-up on the last mission. There was still a bad taste in my mouth from being set up and Nick and Dan knew it.

We landed at Subic Bay helipad and took a waiting car to the Yacht Club. There with the assistance of two local cops, we made our way onto the up-market marina, and found Bodyshot gone. Cursing ourselves for not checking ahead, we returned to the club to speak with the marina operations manager. A little fat guy with a hairline that receded all the way to the back of his head, he really didn't want to tell us anything. Nick slipped him a note and he sang like a bird – funny that. He told us Bodyshot had sailed half an hour ago destined for Hong Kong and that it was crewed by Vincenzo Cruz and Rommel Torrez. We needed to move fast.

"We'll need a fast boat," Nick said and then sprang into action to organize one.

~~~

In no time flat we were aboard Panalo, a beautiful Princess V42 luxury power cruiser moored at the deluxe marina. It belonged to one of Nick's sailing buddies. Nick was licensed to take the helm.

We left the cops at the marina and the three of us set sail to chase down Bodyshot. On the flybridge, Nick pushed both throttles full ahead and Panalo powered out of Subic Bay.

There was still a streak of orange in the sky from the setting sun. I looked south and saw the dark rolling clouds with intermittent flashes of ominous purple lightning.

"Is that a typhoon heading our way?"

"Yes, it goes to show how much Cruz needed to run, no sailor in his right mind would take to the South China Sea with a typhoon coming."

"That means we're not in our right minds either," I said nervously.

"I guess you could say that. It's going to be a rough ride but this is the sort of boat to handle it."

I was happy to hear something positive and tried to ignore the storm threat.

"What's she got under the hood?" I asked.

"Twin 385 hp Volvo D6"s."

"And the opposition?"

"Bodyshot's a Prima Buccaneer with a Yanmar 500 horse motor. She's faster than us, but with 400 gallons of extra diesel to get her to Hong Kong, she'll be well down on knots."

"How long to run her down?"

"With a half hour start on us, probably ninety minutes," Nick replied, seriously hip to all things maritime.

Dan spoke up, "What are we carrying in firepower Nick?"

"In the cabin bow lock-up, you'll find an M-16 with an M-203 grenade launcher."

"A grenade launcher?" I queried.

"Yeah, it can fire an antipersonnel grenade up to 400 meters," Dan said.

"Jesus Nick, what are you expecting a bloody war?" I asked.

"This guy is a cop and probably more heavily armed than us."

Dan went downstairs into the cabin.

"What's that sort of weapon doing aboard this boat anyway?"

"All boats that sail the South China Sea and the Philippines are armed to the teeth to protect against pirates, and Panalo is no exception."

"Why is he heading to Hong Kong?" I asked.

"More likely Wai Linig Ding ... a smuggler's Island between Hong Kong and Macao. I wonder if his partner Ringo Raye knows he's on the run?"

"Should you try radioing him?" I suggested.

"No we'd lose the advantage of surprise."

"I think I need a drink," I said, feeling the need to calm the fear welling up inside of me. Being in the ocean swell was bad enough for my guts without the thought of facing a sea battle and a typhoon to boot.

"There's a well-stocked bar below ... I could do with one myself. Hey, tell Dan to radio Cortez and update him."

"Roger that," I said heading below.

In the elaborately decorated cabin, I found Dan seated at a table cleaning the M-16.

The cabin was like a plush hotel suit.

"Man this is pretty fancy."

Dan looked up and grinned at me, "You should see the Jacuzzi up front ... there have been some serious parties in here," he chuckled.

"Nick said to radio Cortez and give him an update. Want a drink?"

"Never touch the stuff," he growled.

The cellaret was really something, coming close to the ultimate in gimmicked gadgetry and stocked with enough bottles to float a convention. I made the drinks, watching cautiously in case there was another gadget that drank them for you as soon as they were made. The swell was getting rougher by the minute. I struggled up the narrow companionway to the flybridge and handed Nick a drink.

~~~

Ten minutes later, after purging my drink, lunch and breakfast over the side and hoping like hell that was all, I slumped into a chair beside Nick at the helm.

"Nice shade of green you're wearing. It'll get worse if we stop," he said.

"Fuck, don't do that! What with the amount of burly I've just dumped over the side there's probably ten thousand sharks following us," I groaned.

Nick chuckled and then checked the radar.

"There she is, three nautical miles dead ahead."

The sun was real low on the horizon.

"Will we catch him before dark?" I asked worriedly.

"Just."

The answer didn't convince me. The thought of having a battle at night in a two-meter swell that was getting bigger by the second with the approaching typhoon didn't do my seasickness any favors at all. Dan arrived on the bridge dressed like Rambo.

"Holy mackerel, you could be accused of being a weapon of mass destruction," I observed with a pale faced chuckle.

Suddenly Nick backed off the power.

"I see her."

Chapter Nineteen

Dan checked our heading and said, "Better come at her from the east, we won't be silhouetted by the setting sun."

Nick nodded, made a sharp turn and gunned her. This was shaping up to be our Battle of Trafalgar and that was making me feel very uncomfortable.

After twenty minutes with the sun almost lost on the horizon, Nick swung the boat due west and headed directly at Bodyshot at ramming speed!

I gripped both sides of the seat white knuckled as we sped between the rising swells. Each time we hit the swell on our port side it picked us up and dumped us off the top at a scary angle. That didn't seem to bother Nick or Dan with their sea legs but it sure put streaks in my underpants. To make matters worse, a howling gale had come up and white-topped the swell with a fury.

Nick glanced at the radar.

"Is the typhoon close?" I asked him with tremble in my voice I couldn't disguise.

"Sure is ... the worst of it is about an hour away."

"This isn't the worst of it! Fuck it's a bloody tsunami! How can we survive that?"

Before I could get an answer I was distracted by a zing from a bullet ricocheting off the gunwale right beside me.

"Shit! Was that a shot?" I shrieked.

"Get down, they're firing at us!" Dan yelled.

I could hardly hear myself think over the roar of the engine, the gale and the thumping of the boat every time we plummeted off the top of the swell. It was so chaotic I figured I mightn't even hear the shot that hit me. It's times like these that make a mockery of being an atheist because you pray to whomever might be listening. xx

Dan busied himself lining up the M-16 for a shot at them.

Crack! Crack! Crack! His shots set my ears ringing.

"Fit the launcher Dan!" Nick ordered.

"A grenade?" I queried, thinking it was a bit extreme.

"Can't risk it Axis, they're probably preparing to do the same thing."

I took a sneak peek at Bodyshot – we were about a fifty meters from her mid-ships. I could see the two men on board and wondered which was Cruz or Rommel. One of them was on the bridge silhouetted by the interior light.

"Give Dan some cover," Nick yelled at me. "Aim at those gas tanks on the transom."

"The what?"

"The stern! Those big blue painted drums of fuel!" He qualified.

I drew my pistol, rested both elbows on the gunwale, and when Dan moved into his firing position, I emptied the chamber at the target and then ducked down to reload.

Dan braced himself, waited for the boats to level up, and then fired the grenade. It was a top shot – the flybridge of Bodyshot exploded into a massive fireball.

The shockwave from the explosion smacked me in the face. I watched both men on Bodyshot go down. Whoever was at the helm, if he was still alive, would now be dodging raging flames.

Nick pushed the throttles forward and we sped towards the burning vessel. Just when I thought he was going to ram it, he swung sharply to port, backed the power into reverse and pulled up, right alongside her ...

precision boating.

Dan stripped the launcher off the M-16 in a flash and took aim at the stern of Bodyshot expecting the guy there to show from his hiding place.

"When the fire hits those gas tanks she'll blow sky high," Nick warned loudly.

The storm was hitting hard now … waves were pounding us and spraying over the bow, both boats were being lifted three or four meters by the swell and I feared we'd collide but I could see Nick was maneuvering the throttles to keep us apart.

Suddenly, the guy popped up at the stern of Bodyshot and fired a salvo at us. We ducked. I heard a clunk beside me … looked down. It was Dan. He was on the deck grasping a badly bleeding shoulder. Nick pulled the M-16 out of his hands, took aim, and then let go a barrage of shots at the shooter. I covered the flybridge.

I saw him go down. "You hit him!" I yelled.

Nick stopped firing.

"If you want the evidence … you'll have to board her."

"What do you mean *you*, Kemosabe?" I complained. "You've got to be kidding!" I yelled to get over the mayhem staring wide-eyed at the yawing boats.

"Unless *you* want to take the helm so I can do it!" Nick said doubtingly.

There was no way. Dan was down, Nick needed to be at the helm – the rest was up to me.

A big wave came over our bow. Nick struggled to keep his feet with the force of it. Soaked he yelled at me, "I'll get us up close for you to jump."

Gale force winds, an impossible sea – I watched Bodyshot rising up high and then plummeting down in the massive swell – how on earth was I going to time that? I handed Nick my smartphone – put my 38 down the back of my pants – then, not feeling very confident I set myself to leap aboard a boat that was yawing in the swell, ablaze, and expected to explode at any moment with two murdering maniacs on board. Who says I get paid enough? I groaned to myself.

"Jump when I yell go!" Nick hollered.

I climbed up and balanced myself on the gunwale with my heart in my throat and my knees trembling, transfixed on the burning boat rising and falling with every monstrous wave. The spray from the waves crashing over our bow was hitting me in the face and stinging my eyes. We rose to the top of the swell – I glared down at Bodyshot three meters below. All hell was breaking loose.

"Go!" Nick yelled.

I shut my eyes and leapt into my destiny. I was thrilled when both feet hit the deck of Bodyshot together. In overdrive, I rushed towards the burning cabin. To get there I needed to step over a body. It was gory ... He was on his back ... the bullet had taken out his eye and blown the back of his head clean off on exit. There was blood, bone and brain matter everywhere. The fire wasn't as bad as I first thought, but diesel spewing from holes in the drums was forming a puddle on the deck and that was certainly something to worry about.

I'd made up my mind to brave a run at the cabin, when suddenly someone appeared in front of me silhouetted by the flames of the burning bridge. He stepped out onto the companionway with a gun trained on me. My Converse trainers slipped in the pool of blood and I nearly did a header. I raised my pistol. It was a Mexican standoff.

"Give up Cruz or we'll both go up in flames," I yelled.

"How do you know my name, Stone?"

"Same way you know mine, now drop it!"

By the look on his face my order hadn't impressed him. I presumed he was at his wits end and prepared to go down with the ship – trouble was he was determined to take me with him. Well, not this little black duck. I needed to distract him.

"Who killed Chicki Dee?"

"Who cares?" He barked.

"You should, because they'll pin her murder on you along with the hit on Ricky Esposo and the murder of Pablo Cortez!"

"Like I said ... who cares? Bad luck about Esposo – I've had enough talking to ..."

Before he could mutter another word a burst of gunfire caused blood to spray from half a dozen holes in his chest. He contorted like puppet on a string. I hit the deck to avoid the shot he got away as his knees buckled and he collapsed on the deck in a bloody mess.

Nick screamed out, "Go! Damn it! Go!"

I struggled to my feet and took off through the billowing smoke into the cabin. It was tough to see through the murk. I peeled off my T-shirt and used it to filter the fumes. Then like a blind-man I reached out and felt my way through the cabin toward the forward toilet. When my fingers struck the wall I felt for a door handle and seized it. The door opened – I found a light switch – and flicked it on. It worked. There wasn't much smoke in the forward sleeper. The toilet was port side. I could feel the heat from the raging fire in the flybridge above me – it wouldn't be long before it burnt through and engulfed me. I opened the small door, turned on the light, lifted the wooden toilet seat and found a wad of chewing gum stuck to the underside, just as Kitty had described. I felt for my phone to peel off some shots but then remembered I'd given it to Nick, so I ripped the seat off to take the evidence with me.

A loud *whump* savagely rocked the boat and knocked me onto my butt. I figured a gas tank must have exploded. Through the open door that was flapping manically with the wildly rocking boat, I could see flames licking the main cabin and that confirmed it. I struggled up, put my head through the toilet seat, shoved my gun back down my pants and then doused myself with water from the tap. I'd have to run like hell through the flames to survive this one.

I took off like Usain Bolt into the black smoke – the flames licked my body, I was holding my breath – then my fleeting feet struck the companionway. I charged up the stairs onto the burning deck. There, the notion overcame me that the rest of the tanks were about to explode. So without looking for Nick or Panalo, I jumped over the side. It felt like I was floating in the air for an hour, then I was whacked midair by a powerful gust from a huge explosion. The percussion wave pushed me further into the nothingness and I landed with an almighty splash in the water – there was no boat there! Thrashing about under the water I had swallowed half of the South China Sea before I eventually popped up to the surface just in time to see Bodyshot going down. I was cursing Nick for bailing out on me, when a lifebuoy landed beside me in the water. Thinking of a hungry shark admiring my dangling legs, I grabbed it like it was my favorite girl and was promptly hauled aboard Panalo, much to my relief.

Nick got a real kick out of seeing me coming out of the water looking like a drowned rat with my head through the toilet seat. But I wasn't amused ... shivering more from shock than the cold we at least had the evidence – Bodyshot had sunk taking the kidnappers Cruz and Rommel with her.

Dan needed medical attention. I knelt down beside

him, opened his shirt, then ripped a piece off it to make a compress to staunch the flow of blood – it worked – he would survive. But I wasn't sure I would with a bloody two-hour journey through a raging typhoon and seas of biblical proportions back to Subic Bay. My hopes weren't high of being able to keep down whatever was left in my gut.

~~~

By the time we moored at the Yacht Club marina it felt like I'd thrown up every meal I'd ever had – I was feeling crap. The boat had hardly stopped moving when I jumped off the damn thing, fell to my knees in the pouring rain and kissed the wharf swearing to never go on anything that floats again.

Nick had radioed ahead for paramedics to attend Dan. He'd also arranged a local replacement chopper pilot ... but with the typhoon still pounding us relentlessly it would be at least another hour before we could take to the air. The winds were so fierce they whipped the torrential rain so hard it stung my face and made it difficult to walk.

We bought a change of clothes from the club shop and then relaxed in the café to wait for the storm to pass. Nick handed over my smartphone I'd given him on the boat.

"Here, you know we'll need to be even more careful now," Nick said gravely. "We might have just pulled off a trap on Raye but we both know it won't end there – not by a long shot."

"I hear you," I confirmed. "You must be thinking Sancho didn't arrest him."

"You read my mind."

I checked my phone, I couldn't ring Sancho the typhoon meant there was no signal.

"What about this Mayor Rodriguez, seems guys like him need to be brought to justice more than the likes of Raye."

"They call it the Judas belt."

"Explain?"

"A Judas Belt is a fire cracker here, a string of firecrackers starting from a small one all the way up to one big mother of a banger at the end."

"Oh, I get it, corruption starts small but goes all the way to the top," I said.

"Exactly, and Mayor Rodriguez is on top. He's got the ear of the President and is so well connected he's above the law."

"So even if we get Raye and he blows the whistle on Rodriguez, no one will hear it?"

"Look, the system of corruption runs so deep it would take decades for someone to fix it and they'd be risking their life. Every presidential candidate swears they're going to fix it to get elected but as soon as they take office they buy into it."

"So Rodriguez will simply continue on even though he's as guilty as Cruz and Raye?"

"His political position keeps him above suspicion."

I gazed despondently at the storm outside battering Subic Bay and the weird silence to the mayhem the big glass clubhouse windows provided – it felt symbolic, "That's just so fucked," I barked.

Chapter Twenty

Nick said the typhoon had passed and it was safe to fly, after the ordeal he'd got us through on the South China Sea, I wasn't about to doubt him. Within the hour we were in the air headed for Makati. It was a bumpy ride, probably from the dirty air after the typhoon and I wasn't real comfortable with the new pilot – I don't like pilots or bus drivers that look worried. Anyhow he got us there in one piece, and before we parted company on the roof of the Peninsula, Nick and I agreed to meet in my hotel room the next day at 2 P.M.

~~~

Feeling fragile, I entered my hotel room and found Lola in bed sound asleep. Joining her was a more than inviting proposition but I first needed to shave and shower.

With my hair all soaped up, I felt a hand fondling my rod. I opened my eyes to find a naked woman with me in the shower. Suddenly, I didn't feel sick anymore ... Mr. Happy stood at attention, and then quickly found a park inside a comfortable warm, moist pouch and then did his very best to please. I ended up in bed catching up on some much needed sleep.

~~~

It was midday before we climbed out of the sack. Lola ordered some breakfast and it wasn't long before I was charged up with renewed energy and ready to take on the world again ... as long that had nothing at all to do with a friggin' boat. I filled Lola in on what had happened on the high seas and listening to myself it sounded like a scene out of a James Bond movie. She sat there with eyes the size of dinner plates glued to my

165

story with her mouth agape – in absolute shock and horror. I might have exaggerated a few details of the story for added impact but we'll just put that down to poetic license.

~~~

Nick and Sancho turned up on time, Sancho with bad news. It was exactly what Nick and I expected – his task force had raided Ringo's apartment to make an arrest but it seemed he had other ideas and was nowhere to be found.

"This presents us with an extreme problem," Sancho warned. "No one is safe with this criminal on the loose."

"I don't understand," Lola said with a frown. "With Cruz dead and Kitty safe, why is Raye still a threat?"

"Because he has lost everything," Nick said warmly.

I chipped in. "We think Raye is the kingpin of this whole deal and he'd be shit-scared that Kitty is going to blow the whistle on him."

"God, then we'd better get her back to Brisbane where it's safe," she rasped.

"No, that is too dangerous Miss Lovejoy ... this is the very guy that had Ricky hit in broad daylight, that's how dangerous he is!" Sancho warned assertively.

"Sancho, have you heard any more from the mayor's office since you reopened the case?" I asked.

"Yes, I called them this morning to report on the hit on Ricky and what had happened on board Bodyshot."

"And?"

"I was given the green light to arrest Raye on suspicion of conspiracy to kidnap."

"Does that mean we're in the clear as far as Rodriguez is concerned?"

"I wouldn't think so," Nick said. "What we've done has put him in a position where he needs make Raye his sacrificial lamb."

"I can't believe Rodriguez is going to get away with this," I groaned.

"Oh, I think once it's over there will be supporters of Raye who might seek to get even with Mayor Rodriguez," Sancho said with a wry smile that Nick copied.

I got the hint this time Rodriguez might be going to pay the big bill for being corrupt. But we needed to come up with a way to get Raye, and then an idea struck me. It took some convincing but by the time we'd finished the meeting, we'd agreed on a strategy.

~~~

Later Lola and I went for dinner at a Japanese Restaurant in the mall opposite the Shangri-La. We got back to the Shang at around 10 P.M., and were heading for a nightcap in the lobby bar when The Terrible Tango alerted an incoming text message. It was from Ringo, he wanted to hook up ASAP at his club Foxy's – alone.

"What is that ringtone of your?"

"Oh, The Terrible Tango, a favorite song of mine."

"I see, so who was that then?" Lola asked.

"Our friend Ringo Raye, he wants to meet me at his club."

"You're not thinking of going are you?"

"Yes I am."

"Are you crazy? He'll kill you," she screamed venomously just suppressed enough to avoid making a scene in the lobby.

"Shhh," I tried to quiet her down and took her by the elbow and walked her to a seat. She pulled away angrily before we got to it and stood glaring at me with her arms folded defiantly and tapping her foot. I knew the body language – I was never going to win so I tried pleading.

"Look Lola, there are things I have to do in regards to yours and Kitty's safety that come with the gig and you won't understand ... but you have to trust me and give me the respect of knowing what needs to be done. That's what you hired me to do, right?"

"Like what, getting yourself killed!" She snapped.

Now we were making a scene and I could feel the prying eyes from other guests.

"Let's go up to the room and talk about it there."

She surprisingly agreed so we took the elevator to our floor with her icing me all the way. I led her into the room threw the keycard onto the coffee table and eased into a chair dispiritedly.

"At least call Nick or Sancho and tell them what you're thinking of doing," she said venomously.

"He told me to come alone Lola. If I call Sancho it could turn into a shoot up, if Nick comes anything could happen putting both of us at risk. Do you want that?"

"Are you trying to be a fucking hero or something?" She snarled.

"No way! Look, I'm just trying to do what I think is necessary. If I don't show up he'll know something's wrong and that could stuff up our plans."

"And if he decides to hold you hostage for Kitty?" She said bitterly.

"I don't think that's an option," I said warmly.

"So what in hell would he want to talk to you about?" She snapped.

"I'm not sure but probably a deal. I'll only know if I see him. He's got his back to the wall ... running right out of options, I'm his only contact. He'd know by now Cruz is dead and that we're closing in on him – if I was in his shoes I'd try and cut a deal."

She flopped on the sofa and nervously chewed a fingernail.

"If he kills you I never speak to you again," she groaned with a sardonic grimace.

~~~

I hopped a cab and in no time flat found myself out front of Foxy's nightclub. At the mention of Raye's name the big bruiser on the door pointed further down Kalayaan Avenue to another club. I cruised up to the entrance of the Blue Velvet Club thinking of the David Lynch movie and hoping I wasn't about to find a warped clown inside singing Roy Orbison's "In Dreams".

A small club with no doorman and little activity, only the relentless thump of the bass from the disco music playing upstairs hinted it was even open for business. A narrow poorly lit staircase led up to the second floor club. I wished I had brought my trusty pistol but had thought it best to leave it behind in the hotel room. Sometimes having a piece leads to bigger issues than being unarmed.

At the top of the stairs I pushed aside a blue velvet curtain covering the entrance and entered the club. I stepped inside and cased the place. There were two main rooms. The larger dimly lit one had small alcoves for customer intimacy and at its center a tiny circular dance floor with a floor to ceiling chrome pole. It was dark and I could see only one customer in an alcove busily groping a scantily clad little brown girl with big tits that he'd exposed. The attached room had a well-lit pool table upon which two foreigners were playing a game of nine-ball. Next to that a bar stretched along the rear wall. Behind it stood a female Filipina bartender clad in scant leather as a dominatrix and at the bar sat three bikini-clad girls. The decor of the club was right out of Patricia Norris' production design storyboard for Blue Velvet the movie. The song changed to Bed of Roses just as I sequestered a vacant stool and sat with my back to the bar. Seems I was just in time, a beautifully proportioned Filipina garbed in a dark blue string bikini with long black hair flowing all the way down to the backs of her knees, stepped onto the small stage and gripped the chrome pole set to groove. A single spotlight illuminated her and she commenced an erotic pole dance that made me appreciate the Bon Jovi song for the first time.

The closest of the three girls sitting beside me, who incidentally hadn't taken her eyes off me since I sat down, got up and floated over to me like she was a long lost lover. With a devilish smirk on her overly painted face, she rubbed my crotch until my rod responded to her beckoned call. She then whispered in my ear for a drink, and punctuated the request with the tip of her tongue. I swiveled around, called the bartender over and ordered her a glass of whatever she drank and a neat Scotch for me. The girl on stage had slipped out of her bikini and wrapped her bare legs around the pole grinding it and giving it the time of its life. I was jealous and was just beginning to appreciate Manila nightlife when the lights went out.

~~~

Next thing I saw black spots performing a kind of shimmering dance that then faded away to some place in the wings. Nobody applauded. The haze cleared and the snarling sullen face of Arnel Gutierrez came into focus.

"Welcome to Blue Velvet Stone, you did brag that you had the better skill set didn't you?" He snarled waving a Roscoe about like it was a water pistol.

"How come Raye sends a boy to do a man's work?" I looked down at the rope that had me hogtied in the chair. I was surrounded by darkness ... the only light came from a powerful overhead spot. Bon Jovi was just finishing bleating out Bed of Roses, so I knew I must be

170

in the back room of the club and that I'd only be out a minute or so.

Gutierrez gave a nod to what seemed like no one and then suddenly a big bruiser appeared out of the darkness like an apparition. I recognized him as the hulk I got directions from outside Foxy's. He open hand slapped me across the face – it stung and rattled my senses.

I shook my head. "If that's how you say hello I'll be avoiding you in future fatso. What the fuck do you want Gutierrez? You're just a fuckin' coward wanker who hits blokes from behind ... cut me lose and we'll sort this out between us." I managed to squeeze out between tightly clenched teeth. I could taste blood – Fatso had spit my lip.

Fatso drew his arm back for a second whack but Gutierrez stopped him.

"Shut up! I want Kitty ... and guess what buddy? You're going to deliver her to me."

"Don't be ridiculous ... she's not in any condition to travel."

"That's exactly how I want her. You can cut the bullshit Stone ... it'll only get your dumbass face messed up more than it is already. "

"You're plenty tough when you've got a gun and fatso here to do your fighting for you!" I growled. "Where's Ringo? I answered his fuckin' call to talk not yours!"

"Either play it my way or we'll leave you in the street with your wrists cut."

On cue Fatso pulled a switchblade and flicked it open. The effect wasn't lost on me. I got the hint.

"Okay, okay, you win that round. So, how do you want to play this?"

"You deliver Kitty to me, then leave the Philippines ... if you don't, you'll be extending your stay on a slab in the city morgue. Got it?"

"What makes you think I've got that sort of sway, I'm only hired help you know – like you?"

That earned me another slap across the chops but this time from Gutierrez. I moved my head with it to absorb the impact and it didn't hurt. Why do I have to be such a smartass in these situations – maybe I'm a masochist.

"I don't give a crap how you do it Stone, just make it happen."

"Look, you can work me over all you like but it's not going to get you anywhere."

That really pissed Gutierrez off. He opened his 38, emptied out all but one shell, spun the chamber, shut it with a click and then put the barrel up to my right eye.

"You think your life means anything to me Stone?"

"I hope not, yours certainly means nothing to me."

He cocked the trigger.

"If you kill me Ringo loses any hope," I warned.

He pulled the trigger. I winced at the loud click from the empty chamber. Though my heart was in my throat I needed to play it cool.

"I win," I said with a smartass grin.

"Want to go another round tough guy?" He drilled the gun into my eye.

"All right, all right ... that's enough stupid you'll give me myopia," I complained.

"Agree to hand her over or the next time you'll be with your friends Vargas and Cortez it'll be in the morgue. Do I make myself clear?"

"So I hand her over to you and then what, you kill her? You're asking me to sign Kitty's death warrant?"

"No one said anything about killing her."

"Then why go to all this friggin' trouble?"

"We just need a little time with her to straighten out few personal problems."

"Fuck off! That can be accomplished around a table or a conference call?"

"That's not up to me Stone! Agree damn it, I'm running outa patience here."

He nodded at Fatso and his giant hand swooped out of the darkness and slapped me hard across the side of the head leaving my right ear ringing like after a Metallica concert. He followed that up with a heavy punch to my gut that doubled me up and left me gasping for air.

"You leave me no choice Stone."

He mumbled something to Fatso in Tagalog and the big man grabbed at my pants belt, undid it and then savagely pulled my pants down around my knees. He melded back into the darkness and Gutierrez appeared again.

"I hate to do this to a virile man like you but you leave me little option. Cut him!" He ordered.

I saw a glint of light reflect off the switchblade Fatso produced on cue and realized Gutierrez was talking about ending my sex life prematurely. The big fella pulled down the front of my underpants, took a handful of my manhood and positioned the blade under my balls ready to chop the lot.

"Hey hold it right there!" I appealed. "You've convinced me. I don't fancy a gig with the Vienna boys' choir."

"No, sorry – I'm not convinced you're convinced Stone. You can still be of value to me even without your cock and balls ... it's important to make an example of you."

"No it's not, in fact it's totally unnecessary ... I'll do what you want just order Fatso to let go of my tackle and back off."

"I warn you Stone, if you don't comply I'll find you cut off your tackle as you call it, and force it down your throat."

Fatso removed the knife from it's precarious position and I let out a sigh of relief. But another nod from Gutierrez and Fatso gripped my balls in his big mitt and squeezed them so tightly they felt like they were about to explode. The pain was so excruciating I blacked out.

Chapter Twenty-One

I woke up in a stinking, mossy rat infested back alley and when I went to move I realized I was laid on a pile of rubbish and boy didn't it reek. Then to my shock and horror I saw that amongst the bed of rotting food were used syringes. I cursed Gutierrez but that didn't help any. Getting out of this bed of needles without getting pricked by one that could've been used by some aids infected smack freak was going to require some effort. My mind was cast back to Bed of Roses playing in Blue Velvet and I wondered if this was some sort of sick joke played by Gutierrez.

I heard a noise, a chuckle, and the sound of running water – someone else in the alley taking a piss. I called out.

"Hey, can you help me please?"

Two faces appeared over me. I recognized them as belonging to the two guys playing nine-ball at Blue Velvet earlier. They were foreigners and drunk as skunks.

"Hey mate, you look like you've had a few too many." The tallest of them said.

I thought it best to play along and give an academy award winning performance of a drunk. I had after all plenty of experience.

"I can hardly move mate," I slurred. "What's that fuckin' smell?"

"You're laying in a pile of shite mate." The smaller bloke said with a strong Irish accent. "Will you take a look at all those syringes he's lying on! For God's sake don't move fella, you not know what might be in them things!" He exclaimed worriedly.

They took hold of my arms and legs and then

carefully lifted me up and out of the trash. The Irishman propped me up against the alley wall, which I promptly slid down like I was legless and landed on my bum.

"You better sleep it off right there where you are mate," the Irishman said. "Come on Gordy, better get a move on."

I pretended to nod off to sleep while they made their way out of the alleyway but I was wincing in pain with my balls aching like hell. Once their laughter had blended into the sounds of the night I struggled up to my feet. There was no missing the bed of syringes and muck the good Samaritans had lifted me out of and it made me shiver. Luckily I hadn't awakened and tried to wrestle my way up, I would've been jabbed for sure and no telling what was in those things. I staggered out of the alleyway and when I reached the main drag I found the Blue Velvet club was only a few doors down. I knew the Shangri-La was a good walk away – I didn't feel like taking a cab and so hoofed it.

Walking towards Foxy's, I sort of hoped to find Fatso on the door so I could take a poke at him, but then thought better of it – aching balls and self-preservation prevailed to take me across the road thus avoiding his dreaded switchblade.

P. Burgos Street is dotted either side by dinky little nightclubs with exotic names like Ivory, the Mascara Bar and Jools. The bigger clubs have a spruiker at the front door to rope in customers for an expensive drink, a gawk, and maybe a bit of slap and tickle.

My watch said 4 A.M., and that was the closing time for most of the bars on the strip, which explained why the pavement was congested with foreigners and their Bar-Fines. A bar fine is the fee you pay the bar to take out a dancer for sex. Ricky had filled me in on all I needed to know about the P. Burgos sex industry.

Pretty well all the foreigners were competing for the few empty taxis on the street – I'd made the right decision to walk to the Shang.

A lot of the older more experienced bargirls I passed on the sidewalk put it on me in happy-go-lucky fun way – obviously because they'd missed out on a bar fine and were hoping on a last minute earn from me. Nine times out of ten these girls were in the game to send what they earned home to their poor family in the province, who were under the delusion that their daughter was working in the big city as a supermarket checkout girl or something – not a hooker. Ricky reckoned these girls lived in denial. *They aren't bad girls,* he claimed, *just poorly educated and dealt a pathetic hand in life with little or no opportunity. A few years of selling what they sit on sets them up for life back in the province – the trick is to get through being a hooker unscathed physically and mentally.* It seemed to me they probably achieved that by sticking together.

I crossed P. Burgos Street near where it joins Makati Avenue. I knew it runs all the way to the Shangri-La so I was on the right track. Suddenly from out of a dark alley shot a hot looking teenage girl. She accosted me.

"Hey Joe, want some of this?" She purred with an American accent.

She lifted her T-shirt and showed me her small breasts. As lovely as they were there was something suspect about her, so I looked away and carried on walking. She followed after me so I stopped and turned on her.

"Hey, I'm not looking for any pussy! All right?"

She quickly lifted the front of her little tennis skirt reefed down her panties and showed me her small penis. She was a Bakla – the third gender in the

Philippines – a Ladyboy or transvestite ... equipped with breasts, a trained mouth and a penis for those that way inclined. As Wikipedia put it when I checked after Ricky had mentioned them: Bakla generally dress and act like women, grow their hair long, having breast implants, taking hormone pills and make other changes to look more feminine. Some go so far as to undergo sex reassignment surgery but this is uncommon.

"Put that little thing away," I growled. "It's way too small to do anything with anyway!"

With her hands defiantly on hips she thrust small cock forward at me and hissed playfully, "It's not how big it is Joe ... it's how you use it!"

"Looks like it's been used a bit too much for me ... later."

I left her giggling and picked up the pace to get back to the Shang worried that my balls had been permanently damage by Fatso's vice-like grip.

The distraction of P. Burgos Street and all it had to offer had freed up my mind so that the twenty-minute walk along Makati Avenue to the Shang had calmed me down enough to rationalize what had just happened with Gutierrez.

The sun was coming up when I eventually opened the door to my room. I crept in making sure not to wake Lola. Too knackered to take a shower, I climbed into bed beside her. Just as I was drifting off to a well-deserved sleep, I heard her voice groan in the distance.

"Hi, when did you get in? Are you all right?"

"Just then," I rasped. "Sorry to wake you."

She reached over and fondled my rod through my pants. It was like a mule kicking me in the bollocks. I grabbed hold of her arm.

"Wow, I'm afraid Mr. Happy is out of commission for maintenance kiddo."

She looked at me like I stolen her lunch money.

"What have you been up to Axis Stone?" She moaned condemningly.

"I assure you it's not what you're thinking. Someone put the squeeze on me."

I rolled onto my side put my arm around her and crashed, too knackered to explain any more.

I woke up to the sound of the shower. Trying to focus on the bedside clock through sleepy eyes I finally established it was eleven forty. I needed a tub I still stank of rubbish. It was a real effort to get up but after a series of moans I made it and tagged lovely Lola to hop into the shower. While she was drying herself in front of the steamed up mirror, I checked her beautiful naked body through the glass shower partition. She seemed even more erotic when distorted and I felt an urge, looked down and found Mr. Happy rising to the occasion. I slid the shower door open and dragged unsuspecting Lola into the shower with me. Her beautiful robust breasts sporting erect nipples betrayed her want for me, so within seconds I'd slipped my rod into her warm moist sheath. Her pants and groans and climatic surge towards an explosive orgasm was something special. Though my balls were aching like hell from the big squeeze, the pain didn't stop them performing well enough to top Lola up with my love juice. We just hung there in the warm soothing shower panting like we just had a cardiovascular workout – well, I guess we had – only a workout doesn't normally have a happy ending – well, at least for me it doesn't.

While I finished showering Lola ordered us breakfast.

~~~

After my fill, I relaxed in my lounge-chair sipping on a piping hot coffee while admiring Lola opposite me in a sexy little purple dress. Her blonde hair was up showing off her beautifully sculptured long neck to perfection and her long smooth, tanned legs were crossed in front of her. Her open high-heel sandals showed off her perfectly pedicured feet – I wanted to rip them off and suck her toes.

"My feet turn you on don't they?" She sniggered knowingly.

"Every inch of you turns me on Lola – but when it comes to your feet, let's just say they're special to a man with a serious foot fetish."

The house phone rang breaking the moment. I got up brandishing a large lump in my pants and answered.

"Hello, yes put him on ... Hi Nick, agreed, yeah had a little run in with them last night, no Arnel Gutierrez and a henchman, yeah I'll fill you in when I get there."

I hung up and sat back down. Lola had been to the bedroom while I was on the phone, she returned and sat down.

"I'm going to meet Nick at the Manila Yacht Club."

"Can I come?"

"Whenever you're ready sexy," I quipped.

"When do you have to be there?"

I checked the room clock. "Oh, in an hour or so," I said wondering what was on her mind.

With a devilish look in her eyes she delicately slipped both her sandals off, produced a tube of French hand cream and began sexily massaging the lotion into her feet. It turned me on big time.

"Release Mr. Happy Axis, I have a treat for him."

I quickly undid my pants, lowered my undies so that Mr. Happy stood flagpole erect.

"Lean back," she gently ordered and then reached her long naked legs across my lap to close both her anointed feet around my swollen rod. As she worked Mr. Happy with her perfect feet she parted her knees and gently fingered her wet cleave for my added enjoyment. It was glorious – it didn't take long for her to sense I was about to shoot my works. She withdrew her legs, leaned forward and took my rigid staff into her warm moist mouth to finish me off – I erupted like a Vesuvius.

A little later I was on my second cup of coffee when she returned from freshening up in the bathroom.

"So what are you going to do about Arnel?" She prompted.

"If he wants Kitty, then he can have her."

"What?" She screamed in an outrage. "I can't believe you just said that!"

"Wait, wait, don't get your tits in a tangle ... we've got a plan, just calm down."

It had to come to this and the biggest hurdle would be convincing her of the scheme.

~~~

When I got out on the street, the stifling humidity enshrouded me like a wet blanket. I hailed a cab to take me to the Manila Yacht Club. I'd agreed to text Gutierrez the location for him to collect Kitty. He had to be stupid to think I'd do exactly what he wanted, but hey, I wasn't going to question him. Cortez needed to be brought up to speed so I phoned him on the way. The traffic was crook – it took almost an hour to travel what was less than ten-kilometers.

The cabbie dropped me out front of the club. As I was about to enter I had a gut feeling I was being watched and scanned the car park. I didn't see Nick's black Pajero so I assumed he hadn't arrived yet.

Chapter Twenty-Two

I dropped the magic *Vargas* name at the club reception and was immediately ushered inside to a table that had a Wallbanger waiting for me. I disposed of the excess vegetation, eased back into the big comfy leather armchair and took in the panoramic view of Manila Bay. I was just imagining the allied forces peppering the place with ordinance from battleships during the battle for Manila in WWII, when Nick sat down opposite me.

"A penny for your thoughts?" He said with a sigh.

"I was looking at the bay and visualizing the American armada anchored off Corregidor shelling the crap outa the place."

"Over a million Filipinos were killed in that battle."

A drink arrived for him. I raised my glass.

"Let's drink to Ricky and Chicki."

We touched glasses and then sipped our drinks.

"So tell me about last night?"

"I got a message to meet Raye at his club, Foxy's."

"And so you went on your own! Man, do you have a death wish or something?"

"I hear you but hey, he said to come alone ... what can I say it's my job ..."

"So I suppose it was a trap?"

"Like I said on the phone, Arnel Gutierrez jumped me. Anyhow to cut to the chase, he and his goon worked me over for a bit to get me to agree handing over Kitty. It was just like we expected to happen one way or the other."

"It just happened to be that way. Okay, we were expecting Raye but he obviously decided to use Gutierrez."

"How many goons do you think Raye has at his disposal?" I queried.

"Hard to say with big time criminal like him ... at a time like this when he's desperate you'd expect he could call in some special favors."

"So he could amass a small army then?"

"Yes, but it's unlikely. What's worrying you?"

"This bloke Arnel Gutierrez is a loose cannon. I tell you, a wrong answer to him and his sidekick last night and I'd be on a slab in Manila morgue now. I don't mind dealing with Raye but I don't like Gutierrez."

We downed our drinks and left the club bound for Nick's car in the car park.

On the way I asked, "How's Dan?"

"He'll be fine ... a tough nut that one."

"Yeah, we could sure use him now."

We got to the Pajero climbed aboard and Nick started the engine. I had the same gut feeling as when I arrived – like someone was spying on me and noticed a suspicious looking vehicle parked with the two occupants eyeballing us.

"I reckon we've got company," I said.

Nick checked the side mirror. "Yeah, I saw them when I arrived, they must have tailed you. Did you text Gutierrez?"

"Yep and he replied."

"Good, so let's take our friends for a ride shall we?"

Nick pulled the black Pajero out of the car park and onto busy Roxas Boulevard. The traffic was bumper-to-bumper and that turned what should have been a ten-minute trip into thirty.

We eventually arrived at the front gates of Asian Terminals, the Vargas family business. It was Sunday and the container terminal was closed. Nick leaned over, opened the glove compartment and produced a remote he used to command the big double gates to swing open. We entered through the gates and stopped on the other side.

I saw in the passenger-side mirror that the car tailing us had stopped a short distance from the gates.

Nick made a call on his smartphone and spoke in Tagalog. "Malapit na kayo?" He hung up. "They're five minutes away," he reported.

He looked up sharply at the rear-vision mirror. "We've got more company."

I took a look – a second car had pulled up beside the one that had tailed us.

"The more the merrier," I joked nervously. We had everything riding on our plan coming off.

Rick checked again. "They're here."

I checked behind and saw an ambulance approaching the entrance. I patted Nick on the knee. "Here we go. Good luck mate."

We shook hands. I swung open the door, stepped out of the Pajero and stood waiting for the ambulance. It stopped just inside the gates. A paramedic hopped out, opened the back hatch, and lowered a ramp. From inside, another medic wheeled Kitty down the ramp. The paramedics closed the hatch, got back into the ambulance did a U-Turn and drove back through the gates leaving Kitty with me. I took hold of the wheelchair, turned it round to face the gates and waited.

Our hanger's-on stepped out of their respective vehicles. Two of them headed towards us, while the remaining two, armed with handguns, covered them. I could tell by his size that one of them at the car was Fatso. As the other two came closer to us, I recognized Arnel.

The ambulance stopped just beyond the two cars.

With his hand in his jacket pocket, obviously holding a piece, Arnel stopped a couple of meters from us. It was then I recognized the man with him.

"Here to do your own dirty work for a change aye Ringo?" I barked sarcastically.

"Only to collect my property ... How are you Kitty?"

Seated in the wheelchair with her head down, wearing a black broad-brimmed hat, Kitty slowly raised her head and glared at him, "Hello Ringo," her top lip curled into a malignant sneer. "So Arnel, are you going to shoot me right here like you did Pablo?"

"That's not my call," Arnel snapped back.

"No Kitty, that's not what's going to happen here," Ringo said forcefully. "You're coming with me!"

"The hell I am!" She shrieked ... and then surprised them both by pulling a gun out from under the blanket covering her knees and aiming it at Arnel. Before he could get out a word of surprise she fired. The bullet smashed into his shoulder and he went down.

Nick jumped out of the Pajero with an M-16, propped himself up on his elbows on the bonnet, took aim at Ringo and yelled, "One move out of you or your men Raye and you're dead!"

His warning was loud and clear. Ringo immediately raised his hands in the air and the two men at the car lowered their guns.

Cortez and three other cops stormed out of the back of the ambulance where they'd been hiding and took Raye's men at gunpoint.

Kitty covered me so I could pat Raye down and take his gun. It was over.

Nick closed on Ringo keeping the M-16 on him, "On the ground with your hands behind your head Raye," he ordered emphatically.

Raye complied and on the ground turned his head to glare daggers at Kitty. "You've committed suicide Kitty," he growled, bristling with anger.

"I've got no idea what you're talking about Ringo," she replied calmly.

"I'll credit you, I didn't think you had the guts but it's still suicide," he spat angrily.

"My suicide blonde," I fired back at him.

"Blonde, ha! Not Kitty, shows how much you know Stone!" He mocked.

"You're probably right Kitty might not have the guts, but her sister Lola certainly does!" I laughed.

Lola stepped out of the wheelchair, removed her hat and shook out her long golden locks so they dropped onto her shoulders. Ringo looked up awkwardly from the ground totally astounded by her. A woman had beaten him – his ego was shattered.

"You're not Kitty!" His whole body was shaking with rage.

Cortez took great pride in personally slapping the cuffs on Ringo ... at last he had his nemesis in custody. That done he cuffed Arnel, his brother's killer. Police cars arrived to remove the prisoners. I gave Lola a big hug.

"You're a brave suicide blonde," I said.

"Yeah, but a lousy shot."

"Why's that?" I asked.

"I was aiming at his head!"

Nick came over with the M-16 slung over his shoulder like a mercenary on the front cover of Time Magazine. "Glad that's finally over ... well done Lola, your sister will be proud of you."

"Speaking of Kitty, where is she?" I asked Nick.

"On my boat, let's go there now?"

"No way man! I'm allergic to boats."

We laughed.

Cortez joined us and singled me out.

"Thank you amigo," he said with a big gold tooth grin.

We shook hands.

"We wouldn't have pulled it off without Lola's

brilliant deception," I said.

"That took a lot of nerve Lola ... your family can rest assured these criminals will pay dearly for their crimes."

"Thank you inspector," Lola said.

I took great joy in watching both Arnel and Fatso being herded handcuffed into the back seat of a police vehicle and couldn't resist going over to give Arnel a worthy send off.

"There will be a Bed of Roses waiting for you in prison prick, now who's got the best skill set? Huh! And you Fatso maybe you can share the bed of roses with him."

They both growled at me but they knew I'd had the last laugh.

~~~

The Manila Yacht Club proved to be consistent by delivering another feral Harvey Wallbanger to our table. After pruning it to my taste, I raised the glass to Lola sitting opposite and announced, "Happy days kiddo."

"It's a shame we can't stay a while longer to catch the lighter side of Manila," she said.

"Oh, I think if we stayed, we mightn't leave the bedroom," I said with an evil glint in my eye.

As I reached across the table to take her hand, Nick and Kitty arrived. I stood to greet them.

"Well look at you able to walk and looking the complete sex kitten to boot!" I said, and then gave Kitty a warm hug.

She kissed her sister and sat down beside her. I took my seat and looked at the two of them, the physical difference was obvious with them side by side. But even beyond that, compared to Lola, there was aloofness about Kitty, a coldness that was probably a tap-back from a life of hard-knocks in the nocturnal underworld of nightclubs and hoods. Nick might be able to extract her from that sleazy world of bars, clubs and misfits – a world that shines like a beacon in the night to attract kidnapers, drug lords and racketeers – cause and effect. I understand it and can relate to it because it's a world I have to visit more often than I care - an occupational hazard.

"So what happens from here Kitty?" I asked.

"Oh, I don't know. I think Dad wants me back in Brisbane but I still crave the high-life. I'm a lounge singer – I honestly can't see myself wasting away on the Gold Coast, singing in casino piano bars and pubs."

"Hey sis, look where the high-life got you this time?" Lola said wisely.

"It very nearly got us all killed," Nick added.

"It certainly ended the lives of Ricky and Chicki Dee preterm," I said morosely.

"Yeah, well when you put it like that I ..."

She couldn't continue, the tears were welling up in her eyes from the emotion.

Nick placed a warm consoling arm around her and tried to lighten the tone. "How about we go to Australia? Take a few weeks with you showing me all the sights, then after that, well, whatever."

With both girls sobbing, it seemed to me that having Nick around might just be the remedy for Kitty's woes.

"I can't believe a lump of chewing gum cracked the case for us," Nick added with a laugh.

We all joined in laughing – it did seem absurd.

"So what about you private investigator Axis Stone?" Lola asked with a smug look on her pretty face as she padded away her tears.

"Ah, I've got cases coming out of my ears," I lied, "It'll be back to old Sydney town tomorrow for me, provided I've been paid of course!"

"Do you need money or are you prepared to take

payment in kind?" Lola said amorously.

"A little of both could well satisfy me," I grinned suggestively.

A hand descended from heaven and placed a Harvey Wallbanger in front of me that to my amazement was naked of tropical vegetation. I looked up at the waiter with an astonished gaze.

"What happened to the foliage?"

He smiled, "We got the hint you prefer without sir."

"You see my friend, we might appear to be backward but we eventually get the idea," Nick said happily.

"There's hope for you Filo's yet," I said raising my glass. "Here's looking at you."

"Nick do you think it's safe for me to stay a few more days with Kitty?" Lola asked.

"You're welcome to stay with me. Until Raye is locked up and the key thrown away none of us are safe. We could sail down to the islands for a week or two in the meantime. Kitty will be required in court about then I'd say," Nick said.

"That reminds me, what do you have on Raye that had him wanting to silence you?" I asked Kitty now that she seemed more relaxed.

"I know about some of his big drug deals including the one that got Tony Lamont killed ... I was at meetings with his partners Cruz and the Gutierrez family.

"Who is Tony Lamont?" Lola asked.

"That's the undercover name of Sancho's brother Pablo Cortez, murdered by Arnel Gutierrez."

"You sure we can't persuade you to join us on a leisurely cruise to the islands on my boat Axis?"

"Very funny, you should know more than anyone how allergic I am to anything marine," I said sternly.

Lola took my arm and put on a sad puppy dog face,

"Oh, come on Axis, please, it'd be so much fun."

That look had me cave in almost immediately, "I've got a couple of things I'd need to attend to first."

"Good, it's settled then. We leave in two days' time. In the meantime you can all stay at my house safe from any reprisals. What do you need to do Axis?" Nick asked.

"Kitty do you have the address of Chicki's family in Legazpi City?"

"Bicol? Why would you want to go there?" Nick queried.

"There's a little bloke by the name of Carlo I need to look up."

Kitty smiled at me, "That's Chicki's little boy. Sure, I've got it."

"That's easily done, you can take the chopper there tomorrow," Nick decided.

"Man, I don't want to be costing you a fortune, I can hire a car and drive."

"No, I insist, while you're in my country you're my guest, my friend. What else, you said a couple of things?"

"I need to pay Rick's parents a visit in Diliman."

"No problem, I'll have my driver take you."

"Thanks Nick."

Chapter Twenty-Three

I asked Nick's driver to stop at an ATM. He pulled over at a shopping mall and I rushed over to a hole in the wall and shoved my card in the slot. The money was there from Winston, paid in full: ten grand. I withdrew Four thousand US dollars and climbed back into the Pajero.

When we arrived at Rick's parents place in Dilman, I popped two grand cash, about a hundred thousand pesos, into a Shangri-La envelope, left Dom the driver in the car, went to the front door of the house and knocked. I was immediately taken aback when a guy the spitting image of Ricky only younger, answered the door.

"You'd have to be Ricky's brother from the States," I said. "Boy you guys look ..."

"Yeah, people always say we look like twins. You must be Mr. Stone ... I'm William but my friends call me Billy."

"I came to pay my respects Billy."

"My parents are at the funeral home, I was just about to catch a Jeepney there."

"If you want to direct us we'll take the Pajero."

"No problems," he smiled.

He was just like Ricky in manner and personality.

After a short drive Billy stopped us outside St. Peters Memorial Chapel in Diliman. I left Dom in the car and we entered the Chapel complex. A brief walk and we found Mr. and Mrs. Esposo seated in a small chapel amongst other mourners. In the center of the room on a stand was an open coffin surrounded by a vast number of wreaths. I approached the Esposo family unsure of how I would be received. When

Ricky's mother sighted me she stood up and then warmly embraced me. There was no holding back the tears. Ricky's dad struggled to his feet and wobbled over to embrace me as well. I was so touched I was lost for words.

"I'm so sorry for your loss Mr. and Mrs. Esposo," I stammered awkwardly, "Ricky took a bullet for me and for that I will be forever grateful. I want you to know your son died a hero."

I slipped the envelope into Mr. Esposo's Parkinson's stricken hand.

"Please take this, Ricky earned it." I lied because I didn't want them to feel I was patronizing them.

Billy came over, took me by the arm and walked me over to the casket.

We don't have an open coffin policy in Australia and I'm not at all religious, so I must admit it rocked me a little seeing the bloke I'd only been talking to a couple of days ago, laid out looking like a Madman Tussauds wax replica. Even though there was a resemblance to Ricky, to me it was just a lifeless shell. I acted like I thought I was expected to and then bid my goodbyes. Billy walked me out to the Pajero.

"Dad said there was two thousand dollars in the envelope you gave him ... Ricky wouldn't have earned that much in six months. That was a kind gesture, I want to personally thank you Mr. Stone."

"Hey call me Axis, and listen if ever you want to step into your brother's big shoes and become a sleuth," I handed him my business card. "Call me, if you're half as good as Ricky was then you'd be twice as good as anyone else. He was a top bloke Billy. He took a bullet for me and nothing I can do or say can ever repay that except to remember him."

We hugged ... both of us teary eyed. It felt like I'd known him as well as I did Ricky and somehow I felt deep down inside we would meet again soon, somewhere down that dusty dirt track.

~~~

We drove to the Shangri-La. Dom waited while I went to my room and packed. I'd been ordered to pack Lola's things as well. There was a message light on when I arrived. I called reception and they replayed it. The office of Mayor Rodriguez asked for a call back. The clock said it was five thirty, too late to call. I put on the side holster and pistol Ricky had given me and called the concierge. Within minutes there was a tap on the door and I let in a young porter with his trolley to take care of the baggage. I went down to the cashier to checkout. While waiting for the check to be made up I noticed a guy sitting nearby reading the Philippine Star newspaper. The headline on the front page read: Ringo Raye arrested on suspicion of murder.

~~~

By the time we got to Nick's house in Forbes Park the sun had set. It was a mansion, palatial – a long snaking driveway that led to the four-story house snuggly set in a beautifully maintained gardens and tropical trees. Dom let me out and then carried the bags inside.

I was still concerned about the call from the mayor's office and needed to talk it over with Nick.

A maid greeted me inside the front door, and led me through the house to the swimming pool outside where I found Nick and the Lovejoy sisters enjoying a leisurely drink.

"Axis, at last! We had to start happy hour without you," Nick said jovially.

I pulled up a chair and flopped into it tiredly.

"Happy hour, I could do with a drink. Nice spread you've got here mate."

I'd no sooner mentioned a drink and a maid

appeared with a tall glass balanced on a silver tray.

"I hope it's to your liking," Nick said with smirk.

I took a sip and announced, "A perfect Wallbanger – brilliant."

"So how did you get on with Ricky's family?" Lola asked.

"I'm not used to the open cask thing ... it just didn't seem like him there. Hard to take seeing he was only walking and talking a couple of days ago. Anyhow, it was good to see his folks and meet his younger brother."

"Yes in keeping with Filipino tradition Ricky will be on display for forty days."

"Ew, I don't think I could handle seeing someone like that," Kitty growled.

"He looked like a wax dummy," I said with a wince.

"They have to prepare the corpse like that so the body will last the forty days of exposure and not rot," Nick said.

"Doesn't it go off and smell, you know decompose?" Lola said screwing up her nose.

"No, like Axis said, all that is left is basically a shell, everything else the organs, bodily fluids and such had been removed and the body embalmed."

Kitty shivered. "Can we change the subject, it's giving me the creeps."

"When I checked out of the Shangri-La, there was a message to ring the mayor's office. It was too late so I didn't call. What do you make of that Nick?"

"Another reason why we need to get out of town," he said sternly.

"Why, what could happen now?" Lola questioned looking nervous.

"I'd say he'll want to cut a deal so that nothing can come out about his involvement," Nick postured.

"Yeah, I saw the headline of today's Philippine Star newspaper, it said Ringo Raye accused of murder," I said slowly.

"Yeah, Nick got a call from a producer at Viva Films an hour ago asking if they can use his name in the movie," Kitty gurgled with laughter.

"A movie! What about the kidnapping ... and everything that happened? ... You've got to be kidding me?" I screeched disbelievingly.

"Wow, I wonder who they'll get to play me?" Kitty giggled.

"Oh yes, it doesn't take them long to sniff out a good smutty story to turn into a movie ... and they'll get it made while the topic is still hot," Nick volunteered.

"That's ridiculous," I growled.

"The worst part is it will end up some whacky scriptwriter's version of the events with no attention to detail at all," Nick grumbled.

"They won't let the truth get in the way of a good story eh?" I joked.

"Very true," Nick agreed. "It's just another reason why Rodriguez would want to keep his name well out of it."

"So, what should I do then Nick?"

"You'd better speak with him Axis and quickly," he said sternly.

~~~

After an incredible meal with my body protesting that it was tired, I trudged after Lola and the maid upstairs to be shown our respective bedrooms. The maid left us at the door to Lola's room.

"Goodnight Axis," Lola purred and then pecked me on the cheek. As I reveled in a waft of her perfume, she turned to open the door and I took the moment to take in her magnificent form. All the way up from her delicious feet just protruding from under the hem of her lovely long white satin dress, clinging to her beautiful frame like cling wrap, up to the plunging neckline that so elegantly showed off her perfect breasts. I sighed dejectedly at being too exhausted to take advantage of all that woman, and ambled over my room next door.

"Goodnight, sleep tight," I mumbled dejectedly.

When I entered my room and switched on the light, guess whom I found there? Lola had entered through an adjoining door. Without saying a word she turned her back on me, her fingers slid the zip of her dress open to a point just below her waist, enough to show the beginning of her reverse cleavage. Without hurrying, she allowed the dress to fall into a shiny white frost heap around her ankles. She stepped out of it and turned toward me with her eyes half-closed, her lips curved in a purely narcissistic smile. My mouth was suddenly dry. I doubted if I could speak, even if I could think of anything to say.

She was wearing a small white bra into which her honey-colored breasts seemed to be flowing in a continuous movement, and matching white string panties. Her hands moved behind her back and unhooked the bra, which she let drop to the floor. Her breasts were free. The dark pink nipples, I noticed, were already erect. The dull light cast a deep shadow down her cleavage. Still watching me with half closed eyes, her fingers dipped into the string of her briefs, and she slowly peeled them down, an inch at a time, until they reached the tops of her thighs. Then, with a slick movement, she pushed them down to her ankles and kicked them free.

There was plenty of activity going on in the area of my groin. I could feel myself becoming hard at the sight of her standing there like that, a picture of splendor, allowing me to drink in the lavishness of her. She was a woman aroused, a woman demanding. She slowly came toward me, and my full, throbbing rod began to ache with desire.

She looked at my groin, and smiled slowly, wickedly, "I can see you're ready for me? Not so tired after all, huh?"

I didn't trust myself to say anything.

She came toward me, her arms outstretched, her hips rotating in a leisurely invitation. She rested her hands on my shoulders and thrust her pelvis forward a little. My hand reached out and cupped her cleave. My fingers ran up along her clean-shaven slit, slowly opening it up. They insinuated themselves in-between her labial lips. Lola began to moan softly, and her hips moved more quickly. Her thighs clamped my hand, and I could feel the twitch of her vaginal muscles. She lowered one hand and grasped my bulging penis through my pants and squeezed it gently, then releasing it, pushed me back onto the bed.

Kneeling over me, she eased my pants and shorts down over my hips. I lifted my backside from the bed to make it easier for her. She took hold of my rearing rod again, circling it between her thumb and forefinger, then lowered her face to it. Her tongue was cool and silvery against the heated flesh, her lips pulsed gently around it. My fingers dug into her shoulders, as the sensation began to froth my loins. She used her mouth skillfully. Her fingers gently manipulated my balls, pampering the welling flow, controlling it, bidding it not to come now, not before its time. She raised her head, and then bringing her body around on the bed, lay down beside me. I positioned myself on top of her and removed my shirt. I was now naked.

Her vagina moistly enclosed my raging cock that slipped easily inside her. Our movements were quick and powerful. Her body moved with mine, harmoniously, driving up against me, while the moans came from deep down in her throat. Her movements became wilder, more abandoned, her legs held my body in a viselike grip, and her head rolled from side to side on the pillow as we worked each other toward an overpowering synchronous climax.

Chapter Twenty-Four

It was the best sleep I'd had in ages and to wake up next to such a ravishing beauty was a luxury I could wish to afford on a more regular basis. We had a morning glory, which was an experience all of its own, then we freshened up for breakfast.

~~~

It was another sublime day and having breakfast by the pool in the company of the beautiful twins offered more eye-candy than the Shangri-La pool brigade ever could.

The Bloody Marys and the brewed coffee were to die for and the eggs Benedict, probably the best I've ever tasted.

"I won't book the chopper for Legazpi City until you've spoken with the Mayor's office," Nick said. "Tilly," he called. "Bring Mr. Stone the phone please."

The maid, who was standing by with the coffee jug to refill our cups, put it down and went for the phone.

"You're looking better each day Kitty," I said.

Her pallid face had gone and her whole demeanor had improved, she was glowing like a woman in love.

"Yes, it's amazing that a wonderful man and a good night's sleep can achieve more than Botox," she grinned cheekily.

Tilly returned with the hands free phone and handed it to me. I checked the number on a slip of paper I had and dialed.

"Yes, hello, I'd like to speak with Mayor Rodriguez please ... Axis Stone ... private detective. Yes, I'll hold."

After a couple of minutes she came back. "Mr. Stone sir, Major Rodriguez asked if you can meet him at the Makati Polo Club at eleven today."

"One moment while I check," I looked at Nick. "He wants to meet at the Manila Polo Club at eleven."

"Tell her that'll will be fine and I will be with you. I'm a member," Nick said.

With the meeting confirmed I was glad Nick would accompany me.

~~~

Dressed in our Sunday best casual, Dom let us out at the front door of the classy club, which was actually only five minutes down the road from Nick's house. We entered the classical Filipino building that was luxuriously surrounded by perfectly sculptured trees and an expansive beautifully manicured polo field. The interior was opulence personified that totally reeked old money and the better times of a bygone era.

"Pretty fancy club, membership must be an arm and a leg."

"I wouldn't know, my family have been members since it was built here in the 1950"s. There are only two-hundred and thirty-eight life members."

"Would Rodriguez be a life member?"

"No, he's not old money ... nouveau rich. He'd probably be an associate member."

We stopped at reception where Nick made some enquiries and signed me in as a guest. He then led the way to the Sports Café where we were expected to find Mayor Rodriguez.

There were few customers in the Italian style café, with its sandstone brick walls and dark red terra cotta floor tiles. Rodriguez stuck out like a sore thumb. He looked more like a Wall Street broker than a mayor, and his black suit was obviously expensive. His face had a shrewdness that worried me a little and was made worse by the gargoyle-like goons seated either side of him, like bookends.

"Mr. Stone?" he asked politely in a deep accented voice. "And I presume Mr. Vargas."

We shook hands and as we sat a flick of his finger sent the bookends away without a word.

"Can I order you anything gentlemen?"

"It's a bit early for a drink, so a freshly brewed coffee would be fine," I said.

"I'll second that, thank you," Nick added.

He raised a finger and a waitress came running to take the order. After she left, he rocked his big bulk back in his chair like the grand Poo Bah, pulled a plastic dummy cigarette out of his pocket, stuck it between his bulbous lips and sucked on it like it was for real. It caused me to look up at the no smoking sign at back of him.

"Well," I hesitated. "You wanted to talk with me?"

He kept a polite expression on his dour face.

"I have some concerns about this case you that you seem to have handled so proficiently," he said carefully. "There may be some resulting issues, so to speak for one and all, Mr. Stone."

"And what would they be Mayor Rodriguez?" I asked earnestly.

"Well let's just say that I would like to avoid my name coming up in any way, do you understand?" He nodded gently.

Our coffees arrived. We doctored them up with sugar and milk and waited for the waitress to leave. I eyeballed Rodriguez.

"No, I can't say that I do understand Mayor Rodriguez. Call me a slow learner but the only time I've heard your name mentioned in connection with the case was when your office first contacted me after you apparently shut down the police investigation. Unfortunately I was indisposed at the time and couldn't return the call – you see I was tied up being shot at and then had to tend to my associate Ricky Esposo who was busy dying from the drive past," I said sarcastically.

"Yes, I heard about that, most unfortunate," he said blandly.

"Two innocent people and an undercover police officer have been murdered Mayor Rodriguez, and that's sort of why I find it difficult to understand why you'd be worried about your name being involved. If you're innocent of any involvement, why would you be worried?" I asked.

"You're not making this any easier for me Stone," he said bitterly.

"You'll have to pardon me, I seem to have developed an earthly cynicism in the last forty-eight hours," I said.

"This is not a joke Mr. Stone," he said tightly.

"Exactly how do you expect us to keep your name out of this when it's not up to us?" I snarled.

"Mayor Rodriguez I think what Mr. Stone is trying to say is, we hadn't connected you to the case, your concerns should be with Ringo Raye and his associates, not us," Nick put diplomatically.

"My concern is with Kitty Lovejoy," he snapped.

Suddenly I saw through the fog of confusion. Kitty knows that Rodriguez is one of Raye's partners. Nick had the revelation at the same time and we exchanged a knowing glance.

"Let's stop beating around the bush Mayor Rodriguez, you're suggesting that Kitty knows something you don't want made public, is that right?"

He looked at me blankly for a few seconds, then shook his head firmly, "No, Mr. Stone," he said easily, "nothing like that at all."

I stared at him and it wasn't until around ten seconds later that I realized my eyes were permanently widened and my jaw hung slackly about an inch above the knot in my tie.

"You sure?" I croaked.

"Of course," he said. "Let me tell what is going to happen," he said smoothly. "Kitty is going to leave for Australia tomorrow vowing never to return to the Philippines. Simple as that," he said. His fat lips curled into a smirk before he pierced them with his dummy cigarette.

"And in doing so she will fail to appear in court as the key witness to the prosecution of Ringo Raye and Arnel Gutierrez?" Nick said seriously.

"So they get away with kidnapping and murder," I added angrily.

"I'm not about to comment on the possible outcome of a court case Mr. Stone, nor am I qualified to judge the guilty or not guilty Mr. Vargas, but the law of no matter what country does have a way of ultimately administering justice. So, do we have an understanding gentlemen?"

"That leaves me with one question Mayor Rodriguez, what happens if we don't comply?" I asked.

"I'm here to pose a question that is in your best interests Mr. Stone, and I cannot be held responsible for the outcome if you choose not to take my council," he stated dispassionately.

I stood up ready to leave unable to conceal my abject distaste of the man. Nick got the hint and stood as well.

"It's your kind of corruption that cheats this country from ever being part of the rest of the world Mayor Rodriguez. Goodbye, and thanks for the coffee."

I stormed out of the café leaving Nick chatting to Rodriguez in Tagalog.

~~~

Nick caught up with me in the lobby. It took me a

while to calm down but by the time we were half way to Nick's house, after sitting in the Pajero silently brooding, I asked Nick, "What did you say to the prick after I left?"

"I told him we would leave tomorrow provided he agreed to certain conditions."

I shook my head in disbelief, "So what conditions?"

"In Filipino we call it Panero. It basically means two men of equal standing agree to keep their word."

"A troth or something?" I said.

"Yes, like that."

"Kitty can submit her sworn evidence from Australia by proxy anyway, and that should be enough to put those bastards away forever, so I guess it doesn't really matter, he just gets away with his involvement."

"At the end of the day it's up to Kitty if she wants to mention Mayor Rodriguez or not," he said with a smug smile.

I got his drift, one way or the other Raye and Gutierrez would pay dearly for their crimes and if that meant Kitty and us staying safe but still getting the desired result, then I was all for it.

~~~

Later that afternoon a chopper landed on the helipad in Nick's backyard. Dom came along to drive me around Legazpi City.

The four hundred kilometer trip took ninety minutes or so in the chopper and the scenery was scintillating all the way. As we approached Legazpi airport the pilot gave us a flyby view of Mount Mayon, an active volcano – it was breathtaking.

There was a car waiting for us at the airport. Dom got in behind the wheel and we hit the road bound for Magnolia Street. I was in awe of Nick, whatever he planned it ticked with the precision of a Patek Philippe watch.

Twenty minutes later we pulled up outside an old house at the end of the suburban street. It wasn't difficult to tell by the state of the houses in the street that they belonged to the very poor.

"This is it sir," Dom said.

"You better come with me Dom in case they don't speak any English."

The house was run down with chickens clucking around on the front lawn. We fought our way past them, and battled through the waist high weeds up to the front door and knocked. Eventually an old lady came to the door. Dom spoke to her in Tagalog. A toothless smile spread on her wrinkled face and she invited us to sit with her on the porch. I don't think she'd ever had a foreigner visit before because she could hardly take her eyes off me.

I told Dom to delicately explain that after what had happened to Chicki, I wanted to meet her son Carlo. She nodded and called out his name. A young good-looking boy came from inside and sat shyly on the seat beside his grandmother. I held out my hand for him to shake, he took it and we shook loosely.

"Hi Carlo, I'm Axis."

"Hi Axis," he muttered, a little unsure of his English.

I pulled an envelope out of my back pocket and handed it to him.

"Your mum wanted you to have this son, so that you can go to a good school."

Carlo tentatively took the envelope, opened it and peeked inside. His eyes lit up and he handed it to his grandmother. After a look she burst into tears and began babbling to Dom in Tagalog. He translated for me.

"Sir, Irene said it is the most money she has ever seen and she thanks God that you, an angel, was sent to deliver it to Carlo. The money will give him an opportunity in life and he will never forget you."

I handed Irene my business card and promised, "When Carlo gets old enough he can call me. I will always be there to help."

When Dom explained that to them, Irene and Carlo jumped up and hugged me. Losing his mother must have been devastating for Carlo, but seeing his little face light up with hope, made my visit all worthwhile.

I shed a tear myself saying goodbye to little Carlo and his lovely old grandmother.

~~~

It felt as though I was losing an old friend when I said goodbye to Nick at Ninoy Aquino International Airport. Though we'd had our differences, we had been through a lot and the camaraderie that resulted from the experience would stay with us forever. We agreed to meet up if and when he made it to Sydney. He would follow after Kitty and Lola to Brisbane in a few days but for now we'd leave him behind to take a Qantas flight to Sydney that went via a stop in Brisbane.

By the time we left Nick behind at the departure gate Kitty was an emotional mess, lucky Lola was there to lend a shoulder to cry on.

~~~

Lola and I sat together in the plane with Kitty sitting across the aisle from us. Once the plane was in the air and the seat belt sign turned off, our business class hostess offered me a choice of newspapers to read and I chose the Philippine Star. When I opened it I was shocked by what I found. The headline on page three read: Ringo Raye and Arnel Gutierrez killed in police vehicle accident. The article went on to say that the two men accused of kidnapping and murder were being transferred from one prison to another when the accident happened. A truck ran a red light and collided with the police van. The van burst into flames. The truck driver and the two police in the van escaped injury but Raye and Gutierrez burnt to death handcuffed in the back of the police van unable to escape. It would have been a grizzly death. Suddenly I understood what Panero meant and what Nick and Rodriguez must have had agreed on. This was the way it would happen – it provided a safe ticket for the mayor and closure to the case. I suspected it could even have been another of Nick's well-executed plans. I thought, well the mayor did say the law of every country has a way of ultimately administering justice. But I couldn't help hoping that if karma exists then the mayor should one day get his just deserts.

I showed the article to Lola, she smiled and simply said without much emotion, "Huh, what goes around comes around."

When I handed the newspaper to Kitty, we both watched her sink into her seat with relief after reading it.

~~~

The girls left me at Brisbane airport. I sat in the transit lounge thinking of how much I'd miss my suicide blonde and all she had to offer – and boy, wasn't that plenty. I pulled my smartphone out, switched off roaming and changed the ringtone from The Terrible Tango to another of my favorite songs Someday Soon. I'd made it a habit of setting a different ringtone for each case, and I was being optimistic thinking there would be one waiting for me in Sydney. Just then a call came echoing over the PA that flight QF20 for Sydney was now boarding.

The big Qantas jet soared up into the thick gloomy cloud base that blanketed Brisbane like a bad hangover. After a few bumps we cut through the murk into the smoothness of a clear blue dawn sky – I loved that feeling and for me it marked the beginning of a brand new adventure.

❄ ❄ ❄

Thank you for reading.
Please review this book. Reviews help others find New
Pulp Press and inspire us to keep providing these
marvelous tales.

If you would like to be put on our email list to receive
updates on new releases, contests, and promotions,
please go to NewPulpPress.com and sign up.

About the Author

Gary Keady (A/K/A Canon Doyle) is a writer, producer, director, film editor and composer with a range of credits in television, film, sound recordings and composing. Gary has owned and operated independent record labels and film production companies in several countries. He has worked in executive management and creative positions in South East Asian, USA and UK media companies. He has created original programming and formats, and has successfully sold his own work around the world. Broadcasters include *Star TV Hong Kong, RTN 9 Philippines, SBS Singapore, Briz 31 Australia.*

Gary wrote and directed the award winning Australian feature film *'Sons of Steel', and the 52 episode international television series 'P-Max'.*

'Sons of Steel' premiered at the Cannes Film Festival in 1989 and later won critical acclaim with official selection at the 7th Brussels International Festival of Fantastic Film.

NewPulpPress.com
or AbsolutelyAmazingeBooks.com